Yasmina Khadra is the pen name of award-winning Algerian author Mohammed Moulessehoul. His novels include *The Swallows of Kabul*, *The Attack*, and *The Sirens of Baghdad*. In 2011 Yasmina Khadra was awarded the prestigious Grand prix de la littérature Henri Gal by the Académie Française.

Julian Evans is a writer and translator from French and German. His most recent translations are Michel Déon's *The Foundling Boy* and *The Foundling's War*.

Also by Yasmina Khadra

The Dictator's Last Night

GALLIC

The Dictator's Last Night

Night

Yasmina Khadra

translated from the French by Julian Evans

Gallic Books
London

A Gallic Book

First published in France as *La Dernière Nuit du Raïs* by Éditions Julliard, 2015
Copyright © Éditions Julliard, 2015

English translation copyright © Julian Evans, 2015
First published in Great Britain in 2015 by Gallic Books, 59 Ebury Street,
London, SW1W 0NZ

A CIP record for this book is available from the British Library
ISBN 978-1-910477-13-7

Typeset in Fournier MT by Gallic Books
Printed in the UK by CPI (CR0 4YY)
2 4 6 8 10 9 7 5 3 1

If you desire to move towards lasting peace
Smile at the destiny that strikes you down
and strike no one
— Omar Khayyam

Sirte, District Two
Night of 19 October 2011

When I was a boy, my uncle – my mother's brother – sometimes took me with him into the desert. For him it was a journey that meant more than going back to his roots. It was a cleansing of his spirit.

I was too young to understand the things he was trying to instil in me, but I loved to listen to him.

My uncle was a poet, uncelebrated and unassuming, a touchingly humble Bedouin whose only wish was to pitch his tent in the shade of a rock and sit listening to the wind whistle across the sand, as stealthy as a shadow.

He owned a magnificent bay horse, two watchful greyhounds, and an old rifle he used to hunt mouflons, and he knew better than anyone how to trap jerboas (for their medicinal properties) as well as the spiny-tailed lizards that he stuffed and varnished and sold in the souk.

When night fell, he would light a campfire and, after a meagre meal and a cup of too-sweet tea, he would slip into a reverie. To see him commune with the silence and barrenness of the rock-littered plains was a moment of grace for me.

There were times when I felt as though his spirit was escaping from his body, leaving me with just a scarecrow for company, as speechless as the goatskin flask that dangled at the entrance to the tent. When that happened I felt utterly alone in the world and, suddenly scared of the Sahara's mysteries, swirling around me like an army of jinn, I would gently nudge him to make him come back to me. He would surface from his trance, his eyes sparkling, and smile at me. I shall never see a smile more beautiful than his – not on the faces of the women I have graced with my manhood nor those of the courtesans I have raised in their station in life. Reserved, almost invisible, my uncle was a man of slow, gentle gestures who rarely showed his feelings. His voice was barely audible, though when he talked to me it resonated through me like a song. He would say, his gaze lost somewhere in the glittering heavens, that there was a star up there for every brave man on earth. I asked him to show me mine. His finger pointed unhesitatingly at the moon, as though it was obvious. And once he had said it, every time I raised my eyes to heaven I saw the moon as full. Every night. My full moon, nobody else's. Never less than perfect, never hidden. Lighting my way. So beautiful that no other enchantment came near it. So radiant that it put the stars around it in the shade. So splendid that it looked cramped in the infinity of space.

My uncle swore that I was the Ghous clan's chosen one, the child who would restore to the Kadhafa tribe all its legends and former lustre.

Tonight, sixty-three years later, I seem to see fewer stars in the sky over Sirte, and of my full moon only a greyish wisp remains, hardly wider than a nail clipping. All of the world's romance is being smothered in the smoke billowing up from the burning houses, while the day, weighed down by dust and fighting, cowers miserably beneath the whistle of rockets. The silence that once lulled my soul has something apocalyptic about it now, while the gunfire that shatters it here and there is doing its best to challenge a myth far beyond the reach of any weaponry, in other words myself, the Brotherly Guide, the miracle boy who became the infallible visionary, who people thought was abnormal but who stands as firm as a lighthouse in a raging sea, sweeping with its luminous beam both the treacherous shadows and the gleaming cauldron of foam.

I heard one of my guards, concealed in the darkness, say that we were living through 'our night of doubt' and ask himself whether dawn would reveal the eyes of the world upon us or our bodies delivered to the flames.

His words upset me, but I did not reprimand him. It was unnecessary. If he had had the slightest presence of mind he would not have uttered such blasphemies. There is no greater insult than to doubt in my presence.

If I am still alive, it is proof that all is not lost.

I am Muammar Gaddafi. That should be enough for faith not to waver.

I am him through whom salvation will come.

I fear neither tempests nor mutinies. Place your hand on my heart; its rhythm beats out the certain annihilation of the renegades …

God is with me!

Has He not chosen me, of all men, to stand up to the most powerful nations and their hegemonic greed? I was no more than a young and disillusioned officer, whose commands barely rose above a whisper, but I dared to say no to their *faits accomplis*, to cry 'Enough!' to all their abuses, and I changed the course of destiny the way you turn over the cards you refuse to deal. It was a time when heads rolled if men ever stepped out of line, without trial and without warning. I knew the risks and I accepted them with a steely indifference, certain that a just cause must be defended because that is the prime condition on which we deserve to exist.

Because my anger was strong and clean and my resolve legitimate, the Lord raised me above the banners and the hymns for the whole world to see and hear me.

So I refuse to believe that the Crusaders' bell tolls for me, the enlightened Muslim who has triumphed over every infamy and plot against him and who will still be here when everything is finally revealed. This sham of an insurrection that confronts me today, this shoddy little war being waged against a legend – my legend – is no more than another trial on my path – and is it not the gods' trials that form them?

I shall emerge from this chaos stronger than ever, like the phoenix rising from its ashes. My voice will carry further than ballistic missiles, and I shall silence storms by tapping my finger on my lectern.

I am Muammar Gaddafi, mythology made flesh. And if there are fewer stars in the sky over Sirte this evening, and my moon looks no fatter than a nail clipping, it is so that I should remain the one constellation that matters.

They can fire all the missiles they have at me, I shall see only fireworks celebrating me. They can move mountains, and I shall glimpse in their piles of rocks only the thousands of clamouring faces that surround me in public. They can unleash all their devils on my guardian angels, and no evil force will deter me from my mission, because it was written even before Qasr Abu Hadi opened its arms to receive me that I am the one who will avenge every wrong against the oppressed masses by forcing the Devil and his accomplices to their knees.

'Brotherly Guide …'

A shooting star has just raced across the sky. And that voice! Where is it coming from?

A shiver runs down my spine. A tumult of emotion

surges through my being. That voice—

'Brotherly Guide …'

I turn round.

It is only the orderly, rigid with deference, standing in the doorway of what was once a charming living room.

'Yes?'

'Your dinner is ready, sir.'

'Bring it to me here.'

'It would be better to have it in the room next door. We have blacked out the windows and lit candles there. In here any glimmer of light would betray your presence. There may be snipers in the buildings opposite.'

1

The orderly walks ahead of me into the next room. In the candles' unsteady light, magnified by the tarpaulins that have been put up to black out the windows, the place is even more depressing. A cabinet lies on its side, its mirror splintered; a slashed banquette has the stuffing coming out of it; drawers lie broken on the floor; on the wall there is a portrait of the head of the family in a sorry state, riddled with bullets.

It was my son Mutassim, responsible for the defence of Sirte, who chose a disused school in the middle of District Two as my troops' headquarters. The enemy imagine me holed up in a fortified palace somewhere, unable to adapt to spartan conditions. It will never cross their minds to suspect I might be in an awful place like this instead. When did they forget that I am a Bedouin, lord of the meek and meekest of lords, who knows how to be at ease with the most frugal resources, comfortable on a bare dune of sand? As a child I knew what hunger was, what it meant to wear patched trousers and old shoes with holes in them. For years I walked barefoot over burning stones. Misery was my element. I skipped every other meal and always ate the same food, tubers when rice happened to be in short supply. At night, with my knees pressed into my stomach, I would sometimes dream of a chicken leg so intensely that my mouth could not stop watering and I would nearly drown in my saliva. Since then, if I have lived in splendour it has been only in order to disdain it, and to prove by doing so that nothing that has a price is worthy to be called sacred, that no grail can elevate a mouthful of wine to the status of a magic potion, that whether a man is dressed in silks or rags he is only ever himself ... and I am Gaddafi, sovereign, as happy sitting on a milestone as a throne.

I do not know whose house this was, next to the school, where I have been living for several days – probably a loyal compatriot, otherwise how can one explain the ruined state into which it has fallen? The signs of violence are recent, but the building already looks like a ruin. Vandals have ransacked it, looting anything of value, smashing what they could not take with them.

The orderly has gone to extraordinary trouble to brush an armchair clean and lay a table worthy to receive me. He has draped sheets over both to camouflage their scars. On a tray salvaged from who knows where a china plate offers a semblance of a meal: bully beef in jelly, sliced with care, a square of processed cheese, hard biscuits, some slices of tomato and a peeled and chopped orange in its juice at the bottom of a bowl. Our supply lines have been cut, and the standard rations are scarcely enough to feed my praetorian guard.

The orderly invites me to be seated and stands to attention, facing me. His solemnity would be absurd among all this mess if his weather-beaten features did not speak of his sacrosanct loyalty to me. This man loves me more than anything in the world. He would give his life for me.

'What is your name?'

He is surprised by my question. His Adam's apple twitches in his craggy throat.

'Mustafa, Brotherly Guide.'

'How old are you?'

'Thirty-three, Brotherly Guide.'

'Thirty-three,' I repeat, moved by his youth. 'I was your age an eternity ago. It is so far away now, I can hardly remember those days.'

Not knowing whether he should reply or not, the orderly starts wiping the table around the tray.

'How long have you been in my service, Mustafa?'

'Thirteen years, sir.'

'I do not believe I have seen you before.'

'I'm filling in for the others ... I used to look after the car park.'

'Where has the other one gone, the redhead? What was his name?'

'Maher.'

'No, not Maher. The tall red-headed one, who lost his mother in a plane crash.'

'Sabri?'

'Yes, Sabri. I haven't seen him lately.'

'He's dead, sir. A month ago. He was caught in an ambush. He fought like a lion. He killed many of his attackers before he died. A rocket hit his vehicle. We couldn't bring his body back.'

'What about Maher?'

The orderly bows his head.

'Is he dead too?'

'He surrendered three days ago. He took advantage of a resupply operation to give himself up.'

'He was a good boy. Funny, bursting with energy. We are surely not talking about the same person.'

'I was with him, sir. We saw a rebel roadblock, and as our truck turned back Maher jumped out of the cab and ran towards the traitors with his hands up. The sergeant fired at him but he missed him. The sergeant says anyhow Maher's got no chance. The rebels don't take prisoners. They torture them then stiff them. Maher'll be rotting in a mass grave right now.'

He does not dare raise his head.

'What tribe are you from, my boy?'

'I was born in … Benghazi, sir.'

Benghazi! Just the sound of the name makes me want to throw up so violently I would set off a tidal wave that would flatten that damned city and all the villages round it. It all started there, like a devastating pandemic that infected the people's souls like the Devil himself. I should have flattened it, on the first day of the insurgency, I should have hunted down its renegade insurgents alley by alley, house by house, and skinned them alive in public to bring every ill-intentioned citizen to his senses and make him draw back from suffering the same fate.

The orderly senses the fury welling up inside me. If the earth were suddenly to open up at his feet, he would not hesitate to leap into the chasm and be swallowed up.

'I'm very sorry, sir. I'd prefer to have been born in a sewer, I would, or on a felucca. I'm ashamed to have come into the world in that city of ill omen, to have sat at the same café tables as those traitors.'

'It is not your fault. What does your father do?'

'He's retired. He was a postman.'

'Have you heard from him?'

'No, sir. All I know is that he has fled the city.'

'Any brothers?'

'Only one, sir. He's a warrant officer in the air force. I heard he was wounded in a NATO air raid.'

His head is bowed so far that his chin is about to

disappear into the hollow of his neck.

'Are you married?' I ask him, to spare him any more embarrassment.

'Yes, sir.'

I notice a leather strap around his wrist, which he hastens to conceal under his sleeve.

'What is that?'

'A Swahili charm, sir. I bought it in the African market.'

'For its talismanic properties.'

'No, sir. I liked its red and green plaited strands. I wanted to give it to my elder daughter. She didn't like it.'

'One does not refuse a gift.'

'My daughter doesn't see me very often, so she sulks at my presents.'

'How many children do you have?'

'Three girls. The eldest is thirteen.'

'What is her name?'

'Karam.'

'Pretty name ... When did you last see your daughters?'

'Maybe six or eight months ago.'

'Do you miss them?'

'As much as our people miss their Brotherly Guide.'

'I have not gone anywhere.'

'That's not what I meant, sir.'

He is shaking, though not from fear. This man worships me. His whole being is trembling with reverence for me.

'I am going to ask Hassan to send you home.'

'Why, sir?'

'Your daughters are crying out for you.'

'A whole people is crying out for you, Brotherly Guide. My family is just one drop in the ocean. To be at your side at this moment is an absolute privilege and joy.'

'You are a good boy, Mustafa. You deserve to be with your daughters.'

'If you send me I would disobey you for the first time in my life, and it would wound me so badly I would die.'

He means it. His eyes gleam with the tears that are only ever found in the pure in heart.

'But go you must.'

'My place is at your side, Brotherly Guide. I wouldn't exchange it for a place in paradise. Without you there is no salvation for anyone, let alone my daughters.'

'Sit down,' I say to him, pointing to my armchair.

'I could not possibly do that.'

'I command you.'

His face is twisted in acute embarrassment.

'Show me your tongue.'

'I have never lied to you, Brotherly Guide.'

'Show me your tongue.'

He gulps again and again, his face slightly turned away. His lips part to reveal a tongue as white as chalk.

'How many days have you been fasting, Mustafa?'

'Excuse me?'

'Your tongue is the colour of milk. It proves that you have not eaten for a considerable time.'

'Brotherly—'

'I know that my meals are made from your rations and that many of my guards are fasting so that I can go on eating.'

He lowers his head.

'Eat,' I tell him.

'I could not possibly do that.'

'Eat! I need my faithful servants to stay on their feet.'

'Strength comes from the heart, not the stomach, Brotherly Guide. If I was starving or dying of thirst or had my legs cut off, I would still find the strength to defend you. I am capable of going to hell and back to fetch the flame that would reduce to ashes any hand daring to touch you.'

'Eat.'

The orderly attempts to protest, but my expression stops him.

'I am waiting,' I say.

He sniffs noisily to work up his courage, clenches his jaws, and a feverish hand comes to rest on a hard biscuit. I sense him digging deep into his soul to find the courage to close his fingers around the biscuit. I hear him breathing shallow staccato breaths.

'What happened, Mustafa?'

He is choking on the biscuit and still trying to chew it. He does not understand my question.

'Why are they doing this?'

He grasps the meaning of my words and puts down the biscuit.

'They have lost their senses, sir.'

'That is not an answer.'

'I don't have any others, sir.'

'Have I been unjust to my people?'

'No!' he exclaims. 'Never, never in a thousand years will our country have a more enlightened guide or a gentler father than you. We were dusty nomads that a good-for-nothing king treated like a doormat, and then you came and made us a free people that the world envied.'

'Should I imagine, then, that those rockets exploding outside are no more than firecrackers from a party I cannot quite locate?'

The orderly hunches his neck into his shoulders as if, all at once, he finds himself having to carry all of the traitors' shame.

'Surely they must have a reason, do you not think?'

'I can't see what it is, sir.'

'You must have gone home when you had leave. To Benghazi, right where the rebellion started. You went to the café, to the mosque, to the parks. You must have heard people criticising me.'

'People weren't criticising you in public, Brotherly Guide. Our security services were listening in everywhere. I only heard people say good things about you. In any case I wouldn't have let anyone show you a lack of respect.'

'My security services were deaf and blind. They failed to see anything coming.'

Confused, he starts wringing his hands.

'Very well,' I concede. 'People say nothing in public. That is normal. But tongues loosen in private. You must have been completely detached from reality if you did not hear, at least once, someone in your family, a cousin or an uncle, saying something bad about me.'

'We all love you deeply in our family.'

'I love my sons deeply. It does not stop me disapproving of them sometimes. I do not dispute that I am loved by your family. But some of your family members must have criticised me for small things, hasty decisions, ordinary mistakes.'

'I've never heard anyone in my family challenge anything at all that you've done or said, sir.'

'I do not believe you.'

'I swear to you, sir. Nobody in my family criticises you.'

'It's not possible. The prophet Muhammad himself has his critics.'

'Not you … not in my family anyway.'

I fold my arms and study him in silence for a long moment.

I return to the charge.

'Why are people rebelling against me?'

'I don't know, sir.'

'Are you a complete idiot?'

'I'm just the person who looks after the car park, sir.'

'That does not exempt you from having an opinion.'

He is sweating now, and short of breath.

'Answer me. Why are people rebelling against me?'

He is desperately looking for the right words, the way people look for shelter in a bombing raid. His fingers are nearly knotted together and his Adam's apple is bouncing wildly. He feels that he is caught in a trap and his destiny depends on his response.

He ventures, 'Sometimes, when things are too quiet, people get bored, and some of them try to stir things up to make their lives more interesting.'

'By attacking me?'

'They think the only way to grow up is to kill their father.'

'Go on.'

'They challenge his birthright in order to—'

'No, go back to the father … You said "kill their father". I would like you to develop that idea further.'

'I don't really know enough to do that.'

'You do not need to be a genius to understand that you do not kill your father, whatever he does, whatever he says,' I shout, outraged. 'To us the father is as sacred as the prophet.'

An explosion rattles the few panes of glass still left in the windows. Another bomb. In the distance there is the sound of a fighter plane climbing away. The hush that follows is like the silence of ruins, as deep as the tomb.

In the adjoining rooms life starts up again. I hear an officer giving orders, a door creaking, footsteps back and forth …

'Eat,' I say to the orderly.

This time he leaves the biscuit, shaking his head.

'I can't swallow anything, Brotherly Guide.'

'Then go home. Go back to your daughters. I do not want to see you around here any more.'

'Have I said something to displease you?'

'Go. I need to pray.'

The orderly stands up.

'Clear away first,' I tell him. 'Collect this miserable meal and share it with those who think that they have to kill their father in order to grow up.'

'I didn't mean to offend you.'

'Out of my sight.'

'I—'

'Get out!'

His expression changes from that of a serving soldier

to a death mask. He is finished. He has no life left to give me. He knows that his existence, his being, faith, courage, everything good that he believed he embodied, is worthless now that my anger has banished him from my confidence.

I hate him.

He has wounded me.

He does not deserve to follow in my footsteps. My shadow will for ever be for him an unfathomable valley of darkness.

2

I rejoin my loyal servants on the ground floor. General Abu-Bakr Yunis Jabr, my defence minister, has a face that makes me think of a flag at half-mast. A week ago he was thumping the table and swearing that we were going to turn the situation to our advantage, that the rebel hordes would be swept aside in no time at all. Using staff maps to back up his argument, he identified the weak points in the traitors' strategy, placing heavy emphasis on internal conflicts that would eventually undermine their alliance, lauding the thousands of patriots joining us in droves, engaging with the enemy relentlessly to strengthen the battlements of our final bastion.

My son Mutassim nodded as he listened, a fierce look on his face.

I listened with one ear, keeping the other one open for the commotion I could hear in the city.

The general's enthusiasm was short-lived, and has been replaced by mounting doubts. A number of my officers have deserted from our ranks; others have been captured, lynched there and then, their heads put on spikes and their bodies tied to the backs of pickups and dragged through the streets. I have seen some of the heads myself, displayed like macabre trophies on the tops of walls.

For the last three days, as the rebels have taunted us from the neighbouring district, Abu-Bakr has been silent. His face has turned into a papier-mâché sculpture. He refuses to eat and in private he sulks, unable to command his officers. And this was a man whose orders once boomed out louder than cannon fire.

I do not know why, despite his loyalty, I have never been completely convinced by him. He was my classmate at the Benghazi Academy, at my side in the *coup d'état* in 1969, one of the twelve members of the Revolutionary Command Council. Not once has Abu-Bakr disappointed me or been disloyal, yet I only have to look into his eyes to see no more than a startled fawn, a pet more desiring of my protection than the favours I have bestowed on him.

Abu-Bakr fears me like a curse, certain that at the slightest suspicion I would eliminate him just as I liquidated without a qualm my comrades-in-arms and makers of my legend when they began, in secret, to challenge my legitimacy.

'What are you thinking about, General?'

He lifts his chin with an effort.

'Nothing.'

'Are you sure?'

He shifts on his chair without answering.

'Do you want to clear out too?' I ask abruptly.

'It hadn't crossed my mind.'

'So you think you have one?'

He frowns.

'Relax,' I tell him, 'I am teasing you.'

I want to take the tension out of the atmosphere, but my heart is not in it. When I play to the gallery, everyone takes me seriously. The general more than anyone. A Guide has no sense of humour. His references are commands, his jokes warnings.

'You think me capable of running out on you, Rais?'

'Who knows?'

'Where to?' he grumbles crossly.

'The enemy. Plenty of ministers have surrendered. Moussa Koussa, whom I appointed to lead the Ministry of Foreign Affairs, has asked the British for political asylum. Abdel Rahman Shalgham, my standard-bearer, has become my sworn double-crossing traitor, representative at the UN Security Council, mandated by renegades and mercenaries ...'

'I have never been on those men's side. They were no more than racketeers, ready to sell their mothers for a scrap of privilege. I love you with my whole being. I shall never abandon you.'

'So why did you leave me alone upstairs?'

'You were at prayers. I didn't want to disturb you.'

I have no suspicions whatever about Abu-Bakr. His loyalty to me is equalled only by his superstition. I know he regularly used to consult fortune-tellers to reassure him that my trust in him was still intact.

I was bullying him out of irritation.

I did not like the fact that he stayed seated in my presence.

In the past he would click his heels whenever he heard my voice on the phone. He sweated buckets every time I hung up on him.

This damned war! It not only turns our customs upside down, but relegates them to pointlessness. If I choose to overlook the general's sloppiness, it is because, with defections taking place on the grand scale they are now, I need to hear someone tell me he will never abandon me.

'What is that bruise on your jaw?'

'Perhaps I walked into a wall or knocked it on the corner of my bed. I don't remember.'

'Let me see it.'

He turns the bruised side of his face towards me.

'It looks nasty. You should see a doctor.'

'It's not worth it,' he says, rubbing his jaw. 'In any case it doesn't hurt at all.'

'Any news from Mutassim?'

He shakes his head.

'Where is Mansour?'

'He's resting through there.'

I gesture to a soldier to fetch the commander of my People's Guard.

Mansour Dhao appears in a disgraceful state. His flies are undone, he is unshaven, and his hair is all over the place; he has difficulty standing. He tosses a vague fixed smile in my direction and moves across to the wall to stop himself falling. I know he has not closed his eyes for many days and nights. His expression is almost as empty and shrouded in gloom as the abyss.

'Were you asleep?'

'I should very much like to drop off for a couple of minutes, Rais.'

'Do you think you are awake now?'

He attempts to pull himself together a fraction, without success.

His shirt is a rag, his corkscrewed trousers flap around his legs. I notice he has tightened his belt by several notches.

I grip him by the shoulders and wait for him to lift his head so that I can look him straight in the eye.

'Do not let yourself go, Mansour,' I tell him. 'We are going to come out of this, I promise you.'

He nods his head.

'What was that bomb just now?'

He shrugs.

I feel like slapping him.

Abu-Bakr turns away. He knows that the attitude of the commander of the People's Guard is as intolerable to me as the machine guns rattling in the distance.

'Any news from Mutassim?'

Mansour shakes his head, on the point of crumpling up and collapsing.

'And Saif?'

'He's assembling his troops in the south,' the general says. 'Probably around Sabha. According to our sources, he is on the point of launching a vast counter-offensive.'

My brave Saif al-Islam! If he were at my side now, he would rid me of these defeated faces. He has learnt from me the implacable meaning of a true oath of loyalty and contempt for danger. In fact I have few worries on his account. He is cunning and fearless, and when he makes a promise he keeps his word as a matter of honour. He promised me he would reorganise my army, scattered by the NATO air strikes, then decisively halt the rebels' advance. Saif has charisma. He is a great leader of men. He would make short work of those turncoats.

A lieutenant arrives to make a report. His appearance leaves a great deal to be desired, but his fervour is intact. He addresses the minister.

'Our scouts signal that enemy infantry and reconnaissance units have begun withdrawing, General.'

'They're not withdrawing,' Mansour objects, exasperated. 'They're taking cover.'

'Meaning?' I say.

'They've started to evacuate the positions they took this afternoon. To isolate us. My bet is that we're about to find ourselves on the wrong end of a massive bombing raid.'

I demand that he elaborate.

Mansour requests that the lieutenant leave the room and waits till the three of us are alone.

'My signals specialist has intercepted coded comms. Everything points to coalition aviation targeting District Two. The bloody insurgents withdrawing confirms the probability.'

'Where is Mutassim?'

'Gone to requisition vehicles,' Abu-Bakr says, getting to his feet. 'We can't stay dug in here any longer, waiting for some happy surprise to save us. We're running out of food, ammunition and options. Our units have been knocked out or neutralised. Sirte is practically blockaded. The noose is tightening by the hour.'

'I thought Mutassim had gone to reinforce his garrisons. Why the sudden turnaround?'

'It was you yourself who decided to break out, Rais.'

'What? Are you saying my memory is playing tricks on me?'

The general frowns, taken aback by my forgetfulness. He starts to explain.

'There won't be any reinforcement, Rais.'

'Why not?'

'Because Saif al-Islam is too far south of us. We need to evacuate Sirte as fast as we can. That will give us a chance to reach Sabha, which the insurgents have abandoned, to reorganise ourselves and, with Saif's support, move up and encircle Misrata. The southern tribes are still loyal to us. We'll take our supply lines through them.'

'Since when have your plans changed, General?'

'Since this morning.'

'Without informing me?'

The general's eyes widen as he again looks dumbfounded by my question.

'But, Rais, I'm telling you, it was you yourself who suggested evacuating Sirte.'

I do not remember having suggested such a perilous manoeuvre. In order not to lose face, I nod.

Mansour crouches down with one hand on the floor, the other to his forehead. He looks as though he is about to puke his guts up.

'Colonel Mutassim still has dependable men in the sector,' the general tries to mollify me. 'He is putting a substantial convoy together. At 4 a.m. exactly we'll aim to break through enemy lines. The rebels' withdrawal is a stroke of luck. It gives us a small window, at last. The militias have lifted their roadblocks at points 42, 43 and 29. Probably to take cover, as the signals operator said. We'll retreat southwards. If Mutassim has been able to put together forty or fifty vehicles we'll have a chance of getting through. Any skirmishes, we disperse. It's chaos in the city. No one knows who commands who any more. We'll exploit the confusion to get out of Sirte.'

'Why not now?' I say. 'Before the bombing raids start.'

'It will take Colonel Mutassim several hours to round up the vehicles we need.'

'Are you in contact with him?'

'Not by radio. We're using runners.'

'Where is he exactly?'

'We're waiting for the reconnaissance patrols to come back and tell us.'

Mansour lets himself slide down the wall to sit on the floor.

'A little decorum,' I shout at him. 'Do you think you are resting on your mother's patio?'

'I've got an appalling migraine.'

'No matter. Get a grip on yourself, and do it fast.'

Mansour gets to his feet. His face is scored with deep lines across his cheeks, giving him the look of an animal in agony. Abu-Bakr pushes a chair in his direction. He declines it.

'Do you really believe they are about to bomb us?' I ask him.

'It's obvious.'

'Perhaps it's a diversion,' Abu-Bakr suggests, more to show himself on my side than from conviction.

'They wouldn't order their ground troops to evacuate their advance posts if they weren't going to.'

'You think they know where we are?'

'No one knows where you are, Rais. They strike at random and wait for us to give ourselves away.'

'Very well,' I tell him. 'I am going to rest. Let me know as soon as there is anything to report.'

3

Someone has cleaned my room, covered the windows with pieces of tarpaulin and cobbled together a light from a torch powered by a car battery.

Under the couch I use as a bed I found, a while ago, a slender gold bracelet that must have belonged to a little girl. It is a pretty piece of jewellery, finely worked and with an inscription engraved on the inside: 'For Khadija, my angel and my sunshine'. I tried to put a face to Khadija and looked for a photo of her in the drawers and on the shelves. Nothing. Not one forgotten snapshot, not a trace of the family who once lived in the house, apart from the portrait of the father – or the grandfather – in the living room. I tried to imagine the life that the vanished family led within these walls. They were probably well-off people living in comfort and peace, with an attentive mother and happy children. What wrong had they done for their dreams suddenly to be wiped out? I have spared no effort in Libya to ensure that joys, celebrations and hopes are my people's pulse, that angels and sunshine are inseparable from a child's laughter.

I saw danger coming from a long way off, was absolutely clear about just how greedy the predators were, licking their lips at the prospect of the riches of my territory. But what alarm bells could I ring? In vain I warned other Arab leaders, those pleasure-seeking gluttons who only listen to the fawning and simpering of those who owe them favours. There was a full complement of them at Cairo, lined up like onions, spying on each other on the sly, half of them so conceited they could not stop behaving like constipated patriarchs, the other half too thick to be able to look serious. Arrivistes who thought they had really arrived, comic-opera presidents unable to shake off their country-bumpkin reflexes, petrodollar emirs looking like rabbits straight out of the magician's hat, sultans wrapped in their robes like ghosts, disgusted at the blathering eulogies the speakers were trotting out *ad infinitum*. Why were they there? They cared for nothing that did not concern their personal fortunes. Busy stuffing their pockets, they refused to look up to see how dizzyingly fast the world was changing or how tomorrow's storm clouds of hate were gathering on the horizon. The misery of their subjects, the despair of their youth, the pauperisation of their people, were the least of their concerns. Convinced that hard times would never trouble them, they 'dealt with it', as the saying goes. And they had nothing to fear, because they never stuck their necks out or played the tough guy. At the last summit of the League, while they hid their feelings behind their condescending smiles, I warned them: what had happened to Saddam Hussein could happen to them too. In private they laughed up their sleeves at me. And Ben Ali ... my God, Ben Ali! That creep in his big shot's suit, flexing his muscles to his henchmen, then folding like a pancake at the first envoy sent by the West! He sat right in front of me, red in the face from stifling his giggles. I amused him. I should have stepped off the stage to spit in his face. Wretched Ben Ali, dressed to the nines, so proud of his pimp's paunch and willing to prostitute his country to the highest bidder. I have never been able to stand him, him and his mannered, pumped-up foppishness. I detested the way he cut his hair and his cheap charisma.

I was at Saif al-Islam's the evening it happened. I was playing with my grandson in one corner of the living room. Saif was standing in front of the TV, his arms folded, stunned by the spectacle on the giant screen. The demonstrations in Tunis were getting bigger and bigger. The crowd was wild and hate was written on everyone's face. Foaming mouths were screaming for the death penalty. The police were scattering like rats at the inexorable advance of popular fury. No amount of ultimatums or tear gas could stem the human tide.

I paid little attention to the commotion that the Tunisians were making. All the same, I was delighted to see Ben Ali challenged by his citizens. That evening I was the one stifling my giggles while he, in his quavering voice, begged his people to return to their homes. His panic was a treat. It filled me with pleasure. Ever since his bizarre inauguration I had known that he would only fly higher in order to fall further. A gangster elevated to the rank of rais! I was almost ashamed to have him as a fellow leader.

Suddenly Saif punched his fist into his other hand in a gesture of disbelief.

'He's gone … Ben Ali's cleared out.'

'What did you expect, my son? The man is just a pig in shit. He would mistake a cow's fart for a gunshot.'

'It's unbelievable!' Saif swallowed indignantly. 'That's not how it works. He can't leave now.'

'It is always time to leave for those who do not know how to stand up for themselves.'

Saif could not get over it. He kept punching his palm, astounded and outraged at once by the speed of the rais's departure from the scene.

'He shames us all, all of us. He has no right to throw in the towel. An Arab chieftain should never give up. That wet rag is humiliating every single one of us.'

'Not me!'

'Dammit! He's the one in charge. He only has to frown to bring everyone back in line. What are his police and army doing?'

'What little girls in uniform usually do.'

'What a disgrace for a leader!'

'He has never been a leader, Saif. He was no more than an upwardly mobile pimp, ready to bolt at the first sign of trouble. A street thief would know how to behave with more honour than he does.'

Saif went on cursing. I picked my grandson up in my arms and turned my back on the TV. Arab revolts have always bored me. Their bark is worse than their bite.

4

I hear a car arrive.

Is it my son Mutassim returning with the convoy?

I dash into the corridor and down the stairs. The ground floor is deserted. Footsteps are hurrying to the building's emergency exit.

In the courtyard a requisitioned vehicle backfires before its ignition is switched off. It is a pickup, in a pitiful state: crazed windscreen, smashed side windows, bodywork like a sieve, a flat tyre, a wheel practically on its rim with shreds of rubber flapping on the side.

The driver opens his door but stays slumped over the wheel, with one foot on the ground and the other on the floor of the cab. Soldiers drag two bodies from the back seat. The first has a smashed skull, the second's mouth is gaping, his eyes rolling upwards. A third man, sitting next to the driver, groans.

Abu-Bakr approaches the vehicle, Mansour behind him.

'Where have these men come from?'

'They're the reconnaissance unit, General,' a captain tells him.

'Unit? I only see one vehicle.'

'The other two copped an RPG,' the driver explains in a dying voice. 'No survivors.'

'What do you mean, no survivors?' Mansour thunders. 'And kill your lights, you idiot. D'you think you're on the Champs-Élysées?'

The driver turns off his headlights. His movements are clumsy and slow.

'What about Colonel Mutassim?' I say to him.

'He went on past point 34.'

'Did you see him go through enemy lines?'

'Yes, sir,' he says, breathless as if about to faint. 'We escorted him to the edge of the district, then covered him when the rebels tried to stop him.'

'You stand to attention when you speak to your rais,' I admonish him.

The driver is collapsing over the steering wheel. He gathers all his last strength to raise his head a tiny bit to groan: 'I can't stand, sir. I've taken two rounds in my groin and some shrapnel in my calf.'

Mansour gestures to two soldiers to remove the wounded man on the front seat.

'What happened?' Abu-Bakr asks.

The driver writhes, takes a deep breath and gabbles, as if afraid he will pass out before finishing his report, 'When we were sure Colonel Mutassim was not in danger, the sergeant tried a sortie between points 34 and 56 to locate the new enemy lines. We got four kilometres past their defences without meeting any resistance but on the way back we drove into a trap. Infantry attacked us with rocket launchers. Two vehicles blew up. I don't know how I made it back.'

'Why did you come here?' I shout at him. 'And without switching your lights off. The enemy is bound to have followed you. They will know where we are now because of your idiocy.'

The driver looks stunned by my reaction.

'But where could I have gone, sir, with three wounded men with me?'

'To hell, you imbecile! You never place the headquarters in danger. I warn you, if we have been discovered I shall have you shot.'

The captain helps the driver out of the pickup, puts an arm around his waist and drags him to the aid station. The other soldiers stay where they are, by the vehicle, as if they have been turned to stone.

Squeezed into an armchair, Mansour Dhao inspects his fingernails and meditates on his anxieties. Now and then he talks to himself, one of the first signs of mental illness. Watching him deteriorate is hard to bear. I need my closest supporters to display a certain amount of restraint. There is no difference between a man who surrenders and a man who refuses to fight. I would go so far as to say that if the first has the courage of his cowardice, the second lacks any courage at all.

This man in the throes of giving up, this human derelict, utterly adrift, disgusts me. I consider him the dregs of humanity.

In the room we are using as our crisis centre, General Abu-Bakr Yunis Jabr is studying a staff map, with broad patches of sweat on his shirt and under his arms. It is clear to me that he is merely going through the motions in a role he is no longer capable of performing. From time to time he clears his throat, pretends to study intently some detail on the map, leans his whole body across the table, his cheek resting on his hand to show me how much he is concentrating. His little show lacks all credibility, but he has the excuse of not wanting to exasperate me.

All three of us are looking out for Mutassim's runner. Without news of the colonel we are unable to stop ourselves falling apart. Every minute that passes takes away another piece of ourselves.

My nerves are hypersensitive. To be cut off from the world, stuck here like a vegetable waiting for a sign from my son who cruelly refuses to show himself, is intolerable. My fate rests on the throw of a coin that hangs suspended in the air, as sharp as a guillotine blade.

Mansour stops inspecting his nails. He looks right and left, seeking who knows what, then wriggles in his chair, apparently asking himself where he is. When he finds his bearings, he buries himself in his seat again, holding his temples with thumbs and middle fingers, shaking his head enigmatically. Then, slowly emerging from a long inner turmoil, he turns his attention back to the general, commenting in a sarcastic voice, 'Do you see anything in your crystal ball?'

'What crystal ball?' the general grunts, not turning round.

'Your map. You've been stroking it for the last half-hour; it must have given you the answer by now.'

'I'm studying the various possibilities for a withdrawal southwards.'

'I think we've known the route since this morning. Put it another way, south is south, and it's the only way we've got now.'

'Yes, but the enemy's centre of gravity changes by the hour. According to our reconnaissance units—'

'You mean those two or three patrols we've got? They're just yomping about in the dark, if you want my opinion.'

'You can keep your opinion to yourself. You're not going to teach me my job.'

Mansour goes back to contemplating his nails, which he gnaws incessantly. His head hunched between his shoulders, he grumbles, 'We shouldn't have left the palace.'

'You don't say,' the general answers him.

'We were all right in the bunker. We had places to sleep and food to eat and we were protected from air raids and artillery. Look where we are now. A single chopper could wipe us out.'

The general puts his pencil down on the edge of the table. He has guessed that the commander of the People's Guard is seeking to provoke him and so is doing his best to avoid confrontation. It was his plan to evacuate the palace. He did not need to persuade me; it was what I thought too. Every residence where I was supposed to have taken refuge was destroyed by coalition air strikes, including my relations' houses and my children's. In this vile manhunt NATO had no hesitation in dropping its bombs on my grandchildren, shamelessly murdering them, without remorse.

'We ran the risk of getting trapped underground,' the general argues, momentarily impressively calm.

'You think we're safe here?' Mansour insists.

'At least no one has pinpointed us here. We also have greater room for manoeuvre in case of an attack. If we'd stayed underground at the palace, all the rebels would have had to do is break through the reinforced concrete with a pneumatic drill or a digger, run a pipe through the hole and switch on a generator to gas us.'

'Better than being torn to pieces, though.'

I am a hair's breadth from leaping on the commander of the People's Guard and stamping on him till his body is ground into the floor. But I am tired.

'Mansour,' I say to him, 'when a man has nothing to say, he shuts up.'

'The general is being overtaken—'

'Mansour,' I repeat in a hollow voice that betrays the fury beginning to well up inside me, '*yazik moï vrag moï*,[1] as the Russian proverb says. Do not make me rip yours out with pincers.'

Suddenly a powerful explosion reaches us from a long way away.

The general wheels round, white as a sheet.

'The NATO strikes are starting!'

Mansour gives a short snigger.

'Calm down, my friend. You're getting ahead of yourself.'

'Who says?' the general snaps crossly.

'Even so,' the Guard's commander persists, 'not to be able to tell the difference between a bomb exploding and a shell bursting is a bit tragic for a general.'

I am itching to draw my pistol and shoot the insolent Mansour at point-blank range. His impassiveness dissuades me.

'What is it then, in your view?' I ask him.

Mansour answers with an offhandedness that makes me regret that I left my weapon in my room.

'It's just Mutassim. He's blowing up the local ammunition dump so that it doesn't fall into the rebels' hands.'

'How do you know?' the minister grunts.

'It was you who tasked him with the operation

---

1 'My tongue is my enemy.'

yourself, General,' Mansour says with disdain. 'I suppose in the panic you can't remember the orders you're handing out right, left and centre.'

'Shut up,' I order the Guard's commander, simultaneously maddened by his attitude and relieved to discover that it is a false alert. 'I forbid you to show such a lack of respect to my minister. If he is being overtaken by events, he is nevertheless straining every sinew to keep up with them, while you continue to wind us up with your mood swings.'

'At least I'm looking at things soberly. The rebels have turned themselves into arms dealers. They're flogging our arsenals to AQIM[2] and company. According to the latest information, the squads of revolutionaries whom we instructed, gave shelter to, financed and equipped for years on our home soil are now joining forces with the Islamists.'

'Propaganda! Those revolutionaries are my children. They are being hunted down by the renegades. Saif al-Islam is striving to bring them together to launch a gigantic counter-offensive that in less than a week will sweep aside this puppet army being manipulated by the Crusaders as they please.'

Mansour flaps his hand as he gets to his feet and leaves the room, scowling.

'We shouldn't blame him,' Abu-Bakr says to me. 'He's depressed.'

2 Al-Qaeda in the Islamic Maghreb.

'I do not like people being depressed in front of me. Fifteen minutes with that defeatist is as bad as a year's hard labour. He simultaneously bores and maddens me.'

'I know what you mean. But he'll get a grip on himself. It's just a bad day.'

'I shall have him shot as soon as we stabilise the situation ...' I promise Abu-Bakr. 'All right, I am going to my room. Send Amira to me.'

As I leave I place my finger on the general's chest.

'Watch Mansour like a hawk and do not hesitate to kill him if he attempts to make a run for it.'

The general nods, staring at the floor.

5

When Amira finds me I am lying stretched out on the couch with my turban over my face. She is a solid, brisk woman, almost black, with a thick head of hair and curvaceous bust. She was one of my first bodyguards: a fearless and indefatigable Amazon who has never left my side since she was recruited. There is something arrogant about her but her loyalty is unswerving, and when she was younger I sometimes appointed her to share my bed and table with me.

She clicks her heels and salutes. Strapped into a commando battledress, she looks bigger than ever.

'Take my blood pressure,' I order her.

She unbuckles a side-pack and takes out the monitor.

My personal physician vanished from Tripoli the day after the air strikes started, so I appointed Amira as my nurse. We have two or three doctors in the headquarters but for reasons of caution I have decided to dispense with their services. They are the same age as the rebels and too unproven to deserve my confidence.

'Your pressure is normal, sir.'

'All right. Now give me an injection.'

She pulls a small packet of heroin out of her side-pack, pours its contents into a soup spoon, flicks a lighter.

I close my eyes, my bare arm lying at my side. I hate syringes; I have hated them ever since I was thirteen and a nurse nearly left me disabled by breaking a needle in my backside. The infection that followed kept me in bed for weeks.

Amira fastens the tourniquet and flicks her finger two or three times on my forearm to find a vein.

'How many syringes have I got left?'

'Half a dozen, sir.'

'And heroin?'

'Three doses.'

'Are you sure no one is going into my stock?'

'The bag never leaves my side, sir. It's with me when I wake up and when I go to sleep.'

She tidies the equipment away and waits for my orders. As I remain silent, she starts to undress.

'No, not tonight,' I stop her, 'I am not in the mood. Just massage my feet.'

She buttons up the top of her jacket and begins to unlace my shoes.

Women.

I have known hundreds of them.

Of every background.

Artists, intellectuals, virgins, maids, wives of compliant apparatchiks and conspirators, I had them one after another.

The ritual was simple: I placed my hand on the shoulder of my chosen one, my agents brought her to me that evening on a beribboned platter, and my bed unpeeled its silken sheets for our bodies to revel in the intoxication of the flesh.

There were some who resisted. I loved to conquer them, like rebel territories. When they surrendered, inert at my feet, I knew the extent of my sovereignty and my climax was greater than paradise.

Nothing is more beautiful than a woman, and nothing is more precious. The heavens may twinkle with their millions of stars, but they will never make me dream as much as the figure of a concubine. Poetry, glory, pride, faith are but empty vessels unless they help to make a man worthy of a kiss, an embrace, an instant of grace in the arms of that night's muse … I might possess every one of the earth's riches, but it would only take a woman to refuse me to turn me into the poorest of men.

I contracted the sublime illness called love at school in Sabha, in Fezzan. I was fifteen and had spots and a few unruly hairs trying to be a moustache. Faten was the headmaster's daughter. She sometimes came to watch us boys roughhousing in the playground. With her eyes that were bigger than the horizon, her black hair hanging down to her backside and her translucent skin, she seemed like a creature from a midsummer dream. I loved her from the moment I set eyes on her. My sleepless nights were full of the smell of her. I closed my eyes only to be with her in a thousand fantasies.

I wrote her letters inflamed with my passion, without managing to pass a single one to her. She lived inside the school complex in a house with a heavy door and curtained windows. The bars that separated Faten and me were as impenetrable as the Great Wall of China.

After that I had to go to another school at Misrata and I lost sight of her.

But a few years later I came across her again, in Tripoli, where her family had moved to. It was as though chance had restored to me what my failures as a wild schoolboy had taken away: Faten was destined to be mine!

Dashingly dressed in my uniform of a young communications officer, I went to her house to ask for her hand, with an assortment of cakes under my arm that I had bought at the best cake shop in the city.

I remember every detail of that day. It was a Wednesday, and I had been given special leave after my return from England, where I had very successfully completed nine months' training with the British Army Staff. I was so happy that I could hardly walk straight along the road where she lived. It was lined with smart villas, and mimosa tumbled over the garden walls, laden with heady scents. Cars as big as boats sparkled in the sunshine. It was three o'clock. I was not walking, I was gliding, swept along by the beating of my heart.

I rang the bell at number 6 and waited for an eternity. Every minute seemed as long as a season. I was sweating under my braid, and as formal as I knew how to look, at attention, boots together, as handsome and proud as a centurion posing for posterity … An enormous black servant opened the gate and led me through a garden where the flowers were tended with great care. The path, paved with white stones, looked like a trail of cloud. It was the first time in my life I had found myself in a house belonging to a member of the Libyan bourgeoisie. The sumptuousness that greeted me plunged me back to thoughts of my humble beginnings, but I paid no attention. My career spoke for itself. I had started out at the bottom of the ladder and was overcoming the barriers of prejudice one by one. My family had spent everything it possessed in order for me to be the first child of my clan to go to school, and I was aware that such a sacrifice compelled me to succeed against storms and tides, to prove to the world I had nothing to envy anyone.

My old school headmaster had completely changed. I did not recognise him. He did not look anything like the sickly character with muddy trouser bottoms who had once vegetated at Sabha.

He stood waiting for me at his door, wearing a dressing

gown with a fleur-de-lis design over a pair of dusky-red pyjamas. His slippers contrasted strongly with the bright red colour of his feet. The prayer beads he was counting between plump fingers told of the discreet wealth that accompanied a comfortable relationship with God.

He did not invite me into the living room that was visible at the end of the corridor, decorated with brocade and grand furniture. My officer's tunic did not exempt me from certain customs. The master of the house invited me to be seated on a bench in the hall where he would usually receive routine visitors whom he judged unworthy to walk on his rugs. He did not offer me coffee or tea and paid no attention to my box of cakes or my feverish young suitor's air. Something told me that I had rung the wrong doorbell, but my love for Faten refused to admit it.

Her father remained courteous: coldly, distantly, monotonously courteous. He asked me which tribe I was from. The Ghous clan meant little to him. From what he said, he appeared not to care for Bedouins very much. His time in Fezzan had reinforced his feeling of being a city dweller banished to some wretched hole that smelt of bread ovens and goat droppings. Now that he had a brother who was a diplomat, and a cousin who was an adviser to the crown prince Hassan Reda, the desert and its peasants were a distant memory.

'I must admit I am somewhat surprised by your manner of proceeding,' he addressed me formally.

'I realise it is a departure from protocol, sir. My parents are aware of my approach but they live very far from here.'

'Be that as it may, marriage is a serious matter. We have our customs. It is not for the suitor to turn up unannounced, alone, without witnesses.'

'That is true, sir. I have come back from England and have only just been posted to my new unit. I had to beg my commanding officer for forty-eight hours' leave. As I am passing through the city, I felt I had to grasp my opportunity.'

He stroked the bridge of his nose, half amused and half embarrassed.

'How did you meet my daughter, Lieutenant?'

'I was a pupil at your school, sir. I used to see her crossing the playground to go back home.'

'Have you actually met?'

'No, sir.'

'Have you written to each other?'

'No, sir.'

'Is she aware of the feelings you have for her?'

'I do not think so, sir.'

'Hmm,' he said, looking at his watch.

A disconcerting silence followed that was almost suffocating. Having reflected, he decided to adopt a flattering tone.

'You're young, healthy in mind and body. You have a fine career ahead of you.'

'Your daughter will want for nothing,' I promised him.

He smiled. 'She has never wanted for anything, Lieutenant.'

I do not know why I was surprised to find myself taking an instant dislike to him, with his owlish face, his pince-nez from another era and his sepulchral delivery. I screwed up my courage and said to him in a voice that stuck in my throat for a long time afterwards, like a tumour, 'I would be honoured if you would give me your daughter's hand.'

His smile faded. His brow furrowed and the look he gave me almost wiped me off the face of the earth.

He said to me, 'You are Libyan, Lieutenant. You know perfectly well the rules that govern our communities.'

'I do not follow you, sir.'

'I think you understand very well. In our society, just as in the army, there is a hierarchy.'

He got to his feet and held out his hand.

'I am certain you will find a girl of your rank who will make you happy.'

I did not have the strength to lift my arm. His hand remained extended for a long time.

It was the saddest day of my life.

I went to the beach to see the sea hurling itself against

the rocks. I felt like shouting until my shouts silenced the crashing of the waves, until the hate in my eyes made the waters recede.

'You will find a girl of your rank who will make you happy ...' He had once been a minor official who could not make ends meet, who was more worried about the flies buzzing around his miserable dinner than about the kids having a crafty cigarette in the school toilets. He had swiftly forgotten the cheap sandals he wore, day in day out, the figure he cut drooling over a cake some grateful mother had baked him, the pathetic *moudir*[3] whose life was so meaningless that the garish bleakness of Fezzan gave him not a whisper of consolation. He had only had to marry his sister to an ageing vizier to discover, from one day to the next, that he had status, significance, a caste and rouge on his cheeks. You will find a girl of your rank, he had said, the upstart. A genuine disaster would not have destroyed me the way his nasal voice did, going round and round in my head, casting me to the absolute bottom of the pit.

I did not forgive the offence.

In 1972, three years after my enthronement as head of state, I looked for Faten. She was married to a businessman and the mother of two children. My guards brought her to me one morning. In tears. I kept her for

3 Headmaster.

three weeks, having her whenever and however I felt like it. Her husband was arrested for an alleged illicit transfer of capital. As for her father, he went out for a walk one evening and never came home again.

From that moment on, all women have belonged to me.

6

Under the harsh Fezzan sun the clouds struggle to take shape, while an ochre wind blows over the burning stones. I am standing on a rock, a boy in his rags, and I am watching, in the distance, a black dot that appears then vanishes in the desert's reverberating heat.

Is it a crow, or a jackal?

I put my hand up to shield my eyes.

The black spot starts to get bigger as it gets closer, sucked in by my gaze. It is my uncle's *kheïma*.[4] There is no one inside it. Apart from a double-headed Saluki busy sniffing its backside, and a peacock trapped in its plumage like a gnat in a spider's web, there is not a living soul.

Next to an elderly saddle worked with silver, on a low copper table, there is a samovar overrun with iridescent beetles. Stacked one on top of the other, tea glasses rear up like the trunk of a date palm with feminine fingers for leaves, lengthened by endless twisting nails. Away in a corner an aromatic incense stick is smouldering, its smoke scoring the gloom with curling swirls.

---

4 Bedouin tent.

In the buzzing silence of the desert's crucible, the only sound is the creaking of a pulley.

Attached to the tent's central pole, a lavish picture frame twists slowly on its axis. It is not a pulley creaking, but the cord from which the frame is hanging. The frame is empty.

I am afraid.

My skin is covered in goose bumps.

Urged on by a mysterious instinct, I place a leg into the frame and bring the other in behind it, as if I was going through a mirror. I am surprised to find myself sitting in the middle of a crowd of children in rags, stumbling through their verses and wagging their heads above their tablets. I recognise the Koranic school I went to when I was seven, with its mud walls and ceiling of worm-eaten beams. Muffled in a green coat, his face framed by wild hair, the sheikh is dozing on his cushion, lulled by his pupils' discordant chorus. Whenever the clamour subsides a fraction, he lands his rod on the shoulder of the nearest unfortunate to revive the general enthusiasm and dozes off again.

The sheikh loathed the agitators who droned out their verses and sniggered in secret. When he got one of them in his clutches, he would stop the class, order us to form a circle around the miscreant and make us witness a terrible session of *falaqa*.[5] The punishment

---

5 Foot whipping.

would traumatise me for a long time.

Suddenly the sheikh wakes up and his look fastens itself to me like a bird of prey. Why aren't you reciting like your fellow pupils? What have you done with your tablet? Have you renounced your religion, you little dog? he shouts, raising himself in a surge of indignation. Like Moses, he throws his rod to the ground where it is transformed into a dreadful black snake, every one of its scales quivering, its forked tongue like a flame flickering up from hell.

My heart almost stops when I see that the sheikh is really Vincent van Gogh in disguise.

I wake with a start, my chest tight, my throat parched. I am in the bedroom upstairs, on the couch I use for a bed.

Amira has gone.

I sit up and put my head in my hands, overwhelmed by my nightmare … Usually my fix sends me into a magnificent, restorative sleep. But for several weeks now it has been the same dream over and over again, turning my rare moments of respite upside down.

My Vincent van Gogh thing goes back to when I was at the lycée. One day, leafing through an illustrated book I had borrowed from a classmate, I stumbled on a self-portrait by the painter. Even now I cannot explain what took hold of me that day. I had never heard of van Gogh.

I remember: I was literally hypnotised by him. His forehead was half hidden by a wild, dreadful haircut, his mutilated ear was covered with a bandage, and his expression was evasive: he looked as though he regretted having come into this world. On the wall behind him was a Japanese print. The painter had turned his back on it. He was standing, bundled up in his nasty green coat, indecisive, in the middle of his cold, seedy studio.

That image has never left me. It is embedded deep in my subconscious and, like a sleeper agent, every time some great event is imminent it returns to haunt my dreams. I have never known why. I even consulted an imam from Arabia who was celebrated for his interpretations of dreams, without success.

I have little in common with van Gogh, except perhaps for the wretchedness that I suffered as a child and that finished him off, among his canvases that never paid him enough for a square meal and that sell for obscene sums of money today. I cannot see the slightest connection that could justify this doomed painter's repeated intrusion into my life, yet I am convinced that there is an explanation somewhere.

Apart from oriental music, I have very little interest in the arts. I would even admit to harbouring a certain disdain for contemporary painters: they seem subversive in the same way politically minded poets are, not always inspired and without real magic. They are more the result of fashion, a way (like any other way) of persuading people that decadence is a kind of revolutionary transcendence, that some vulgar red line on a canvas can single-handedly raise ordinary people to the ranks of the initiated, because in that space where all appreciation is conventional, arbitrary and without specific proven parameters, it is the signature that authenticates the talent and not the other way round. Of course, to look as if I was enjoying myself on official visits to the West, I occasionally feigned a general bliss looking at a fresco or listening to Mozart – whose much praised genius has never once managed to pull at my heartstrings; for me nothing comes close to the splendour of a Bedouin tent pitched out in the middle of the desert, and no symphony is equal to the whispering of the wind on a dune it has created. Yet by some mysterious quirk of fate Vincent van Gogh, who does not belong to my culture or to my world, goes on exercising on me an unfathomable fascination, part fear, part curiosity.

The night before the *coup d'état* – 31 August 1969 – while my officers were putting the finishing touches to the assault operation timed for King Idris's absence abroad for medical treatment, I was in my room, totally stressed out. Van Gogh was there, in his gilded frame; he did not let me out of his sight. I tossed and turned in bed, put a pillow over my head, all in vain; the ghost refused to fade away. When the telephone rang on my bedside table, the painter leapt out of his canvas and threw himself at me, his green overcoat teeming with bats. I woke up screaming, soaked in sweat. Mission accomplished! the voice at the other end said. The crown prince has abdicated without resistance. The king is already aware that it is not in his interests to return to the country. At dawn with my troops I took over the radio station in Benghazi to announce to the people that the villainous monarchy that had sucked the nation's lifeblood was dead and that the Libyan Arab Republic had just been born.

A few months later, galvanised by my people's demands, I began to reflect on another coup that would give me greater visibility on the international stage. I wavered between expelling all British troops from the country or taking back Wheelus Air Base from the Americans ... One night van Gogh came back to terrify me in my sleep, and in the morning, despite my advisers' well-argued reservations, my mind was made up: no more Crusaders in the sacred lands of Omar Mukhtar.

In August 1975 it was again van Gogh who alerted me, in a dream of unusual violence, to the conspiracy being hatched against me by two of my best friends and confidants, Beshir al-Saghir Hawady and Omar al-Meheishy. I foiled the would-be coup with some style, purging the Revolutionary Command Council the way you lance a boil.

Each time the doomed painter made an appearance in

my dreams or thoughts, History added another stone to the Gaddafi edifice.

I have often wondered whether my Green Book and the colour I chose for the new Libyan national flag were inspired by the green of van Gogh's overcoat.

7

Someone is knocking at the door.

It is Mansour Dhao, come to redeem himself ...
What is he worth now, at wartime prices? A bullet?
Less than that. A pair of pliers, a blunt knife, a hemp
rope would be more than generous. The commander
of my People's Guard, the terrible Mansour Dhao,
impeccably turned out, attentive to the smallest detail
of his martial appearance, and here he is letting himself
go completely, unshaven, looking like a tramp, in a shirt
with a filthy collar and with his shoelaces undone. A
shadow of himself, of which appears to be nothing but a
distant memory. His gaze, which once saw further than
the horizon, can barely travel past his eyelashes now.

I am sad for him, and for myself: my right hand of
steel is limp and useless.

There was a time when nothing escaped his vigilance.
He knew everything that went on, down to the moans
of the virgins I deflowered between two shots of heroin.
Back then Mansour was my sword of Damocles. He
kept watch on the fruit and the orchard, and could tell a
bad apple before it appeared. He left nothing to chance.

His agents were hand-picked. At the slightest suspicion they struck; suspects vanished into thin air faster than a puff of smoke, and I could enjoy my nights in complete peace.

'Don't be angry with me, Rais. I haven't taken my medication for weeks.'

He has hidden from me the fact that he is on medication. And there I was, thinking him unassailable. He looked as if he had never known illness or fatigue. I had even had my best men tail him – his charisma and authority as head of the People's Guard made him a potential rival. Power is hallucinogenic, so you are never safe from others' murderous daydreams. It is one short step from the barracks to the presidential palace, and overarching ambition dwarfs the risks ... But I had grossly misjudged Mansour: he would have cut his mother's throat without hesitation if she had ever bothered me.

I gesture to him to sit down.

'I prefer to stand.'

'I appreciate the effort you are making,' I tell him ironically.

'I'm furious with myself.'

'You are wrong to upset yourself over a moment's weakness. I too have a heart beating in here.'

'Your regard for me is worth more than all the world's honours.'

'You deserve it … You are a brave man. You prove it by staying with me.'

'Only rats desert the sinking ship.'

'I am merely a ship to you?'

'That's not what I meant.'

I look hard at him. He swallows, embarrassed. He came to make amends for his attitude earlier and he realises that he is compounding his errors.

'I wonder if I'd have done better to stay downstairs.'

'An excellent question.'

The coldness of my tone crushes him. He nods, his head lowered, and shuffles to the door.

'I did not give you permission to go.'

He hovers with his hand on the door.

'Come back, you fool.'

He turns round. The trembling of his lips makes his beard quiver.

'I feel vulgar, wretched and unworthy to stand in front of you.'

'What has got into you, for pity's sake? Is it the jackals roaming the streets outside who have made you lose your nerve, or are you just undecided whether to surrender or kill yourself?'

'I'm too religious to think of suicide, Rais. As for saving my skin, I've had plenty of opportunities to do it. They offered me a gold-plated exile in return for agreeing to surrender. If I've stayed, it is because there is no exile more precious than the shade you cast. You are the finest thing that has happened to me. To die for you is an honour and a duty.'

'I am happy to see my Mansour again.'

My compliment emboldens him. He comes back towards me, seized with feverish energy.

'I shall prove to you that I am the same man, that this war is just a smokescreen and soon enlightenment will spread over the whole of Libya. I shall exterminate to the last man the barbarians who jeer at you and I shall make of their skin a red carpet on which you will walk straight back to your throne.'

'There will be no shipwreck, Mansour. It is not just anyone who is at the tiller. We must hold out a few days longer, that is all. Our people will come back to their senses. They will realise that it is Al-Qaeda which is behind this whole performance. Trust me. It is only a matter of time before we shall string up publicly every one of those vultures who are looting, raping and murdering in the name of God.'

He finally sits down in the chair I offered him, confident that I have forgiven him. He is not smiling yet, but his eyes have regained a modicum of alertness.

I let him recover his spirits before I go on.

'I have had a dream, Mansour. A premonition.'

'I remember the one you had before the invasion of Iraq. You foresaw everything.'

'Well, be reassured. The dream that came to me has given me comfort: we shall have won by the end of October.'

'I cannot picture Libya without you in command, Rais. It makes no sense.'

His voice is too soft – hardly more than a sigh – for his words to have an impact on me. He is as yet still no more than a solitary rush light; as it lights, it goes out. His previous panache is now wrapped in misery, like an old canvas shroud on a lifeless corpse.

I pick up my Koran, lying on the couch's armrest, open it at random and start reading. My Guard commander is motionless. He sits on the edge of his chair, looking vacant. I read one verse, then another and another … Mansour cannot make up his mind to leave.

I put the Koran down.

'Do you wish to tell me something?'

He starts.

'I … I didn't hear what you said.'

'I asked you if you had something to tell me.'

'No, no …'

'Are you sure?'

'Yes …'

'In that case, why are you still here?'

'I feel good when I'm with you.'

I give him a sidelong look. He tries to turn away and does not succeed.

'No letting yourself go, Mansour. Show some backbone, for pity's sake! You are very close to losing it completely.'

His head lolls.

He is seriously beginning to worry me.

'What are you thinking about?'

'About waking up, Brotherly Guide.'

'You are awake.'

He rummages in his beard, smooths the bridge of his nose and scratches his ear. I have the feeling he may be about to die on me.

'What do you intend to do when we have dealt with this stupid revolt?' I ask him, to lighten the atmosphere.

'Go home,' he says spontaneously, as though he was just waiting for the opportunity to express a very dear wish he had never revealed to anyone.

'And then?'

'Stay there ...'

'At home?'

'Yes, at home.'

'Truly?'

'Truly.'

'You will not command my People's Guard any more?'

'You'll find someone else.'

'It is you I want, Mansour.'

He shakes his head.

'The responsibility has become too great for me, Rais. I don't have the strength to carry any more than the shirt on my back now, Rais. I'm throwing in the towel.'

'To pick up a dishcloth instead?'

'Why not? I feel like retiring. I'll spend my mornings pottering in my garden and my afternoons praying to be forgiven for the bad things I have done.'

'Have you done bad things, Mansour?'

'I must have done. No authority is innocent of abuse. There must have been times when, unknown to me, I was unjust and cruel.'

I cannot stand the tone of his voice.

'Do you think I have been unjust and cruel?'

'I'm talking about myself, Rais.'

'Look me in the eye when I ask you a question!'

My shout nearly finishes him off.

'Have I been unjust and cruel, Mansour?'

His throat tightens. He does not answer.

'Go on, speak. I order you to tell me the truth. I shall not be angry with you, I promise. I want to know so that in future I shall not find myself with a rebellion on my hands.'

'Rais …'

'Have I been at fault where my people are concerned?' I yell at him.

'God alone is infallible,' he blurts out.

Suddenly, it is as though I no longer recognise where

I am or where I have come from. I am beside myself, no longer there, outraged, violated, crucified on burning altars. Without knowing what I am doing, I draw myself up in front of my Guard commander, hands like claws, ready to tear him to pieces. An uncontainable fury has sucked all the breath out of me. I am suffocating.

'You piece of shit!'

'You promised not to lose your temper, Rais.'

'Go to the Devil! Yesterday you were stuffing yourself at my banquets, and today you have decided you want to bite the hand that fed you. Suddenly the soldier is full of remorse and begging for absolution. You did your duty, you cretin. There is no such thing as scruples for anyone who defends their country. Collateral damage is part of war. Emotions have no place in affairs of state and mistakes do not count ... What do people actually condemn me for? The Lockerbie bombing and UTA 772? It was the Americans who started it. They bombed my palace, killed my adopted daughter. They launched their cowardly Operation El Dorado Canyon against my aerial strike force at Mitiga. Not to mention the embargoes, my being demonised and ostracised on the international stage. Did they think I was going to thank them for that? ... What else do they condemn me for? The killings at Abu Salim?[6] All I did was rid our nation of some appalling vermin, a bunch of crazed visionaries

---

[6] Around 1,270 prisoners were massacred at Abu Salim prison in Tripoli in 1996.

who had dedicated themselves to terrorism. They were mutineers who threatened the country's stability. Do people have any idea of the chaos those savages could have caused if they had got out? Look how Algeria descended into horror the very night that thousands of prisoners broke out from Lambaesis. Everyone knows what happened: a decade of terror and massacres. I was determined that my country would not suffer the same fate.'

I thump my fist on the couch's armrest.

'Our country was in the firing line, Mansour. Every day. Our enemies were trying to undermine every initiative we took, by every possible means. Including our own officials. Remember the brothers I took under my wing, the brothers I showered with medals and promotions, privileges and honours. They were treated better than kings. My largesse was not enough. They wanted even more, they wanted my head on a silver platter. You think I was wrong to execute them? You think I did the wrong thing? Everything has its price, Mansour. Loyalty as much as betrayal. The crocodile never softens when you wipe its tears. It was them or me, the Crusaders' interests or Libya's interests. When I think how my gallant comrades-in-arms, the ones who risked their lives helping me overthrow that good-for-nothing king Idris, let themselves be enticed by the imperialists' promises and did not hesitate to plot against me, against the Libyan people, against the eternal homeland … when I think about those traitors I tell myself I was not harsh enough, I should have been fiercer, more cruel. It is because my paternal side got the better of my sovereign's implacability that I have an insurrection on my hands today. I should have liquidated half my people so that the other half could be safe, so that every man could live untroubled wherever he found himself, whatever he was doing.'

I seize him by the collar and lift him up. My saliva spatters his face. He is at arm's length, trembling, not knowing where to look. He would slip down like a rag doll if I let him go.

'Look where we are now. The coalition is all over us. Countries that have never had a problem with us are burying us under their bombs. Even Qatar came to the party. And what do the Arab nations do? Where are they? They toast our plight. They make preparations for our funerals.'

'What were you expecting?' he suddenly rails, knocking my arms away. 'That they'd come to your rescue with trumpets and flags?'

I am shocked. Mansour Dhao has dared to raise his voice, and his hand, to me. He has hurt my wrists. I step back, disbelieving. He stares at me with a baleful expression, his face flushed, his nostrils twitching.

'I don't give a shit about the Arabs,' he thunders,

his mouth foaming. 'It's you yourself who made them behave that way towards us. You scorned them, lambasted them, humiliated them. You called them flea-ridden animals led by fawning curs. It's completely logical for them to be delighted by our collapse.'

I remain speechless, not knowing any more whether I am dreaming or hallucinating. It is the first time since I was at the Academy that an officer has treated me disrespectfully. I am close to becoming apoplectic.

Mansour does not recover his composure. He is trembling with fury and rancour.

He points at the window.

'What's happening out there, Rais? What's that, that noise? The people serenading you?'

He rushes to the window and jabs his finger at the cloth covering the panes.

'What can you hear, Rais?'

'What am I supposed to hear, moron?'

'Another version of events. A different tune from the toadying of your arse-kissers and the honeyed reports of your staff officers. The fairy tales are over – all the "it's going swimmingly" and the "*tout va très bien, madame la marquise*". Out there is a raging populace ...'

'Out there is Al-Qaeda—'

'How many Al-Qaeda are there? Five hundred, a thousand, two thousand? So who are the thousands of savages who are ravaging our cities, murdering our old people, disembowelling our pregnant women and smashing in our children's skulls with their rifle butts? They are Libyans, Rais. Libyans like you and me, who only yesterday were acclaiming you and today are calling for your head.'

He rushes back, like a boomerang.

'Why, Rais? Why this turnaround? What happened to turn the lambs into hyenas, to make the children eat their father? ... Yes, Brotherly Guide, we were at fault. We behaved badly. You were undoubtedly thinking of the good of the nation, but what did you know of the nation itself? There's no smoke without fire, Brotherly Guide. We haven't got our backs to the wall by accident. The massacres and destruction going on out there aren't happening by magic, they're the direct result of our mistakes.'

I am so shocked by the words of my commander of the People's Guard that my knees threaten to give way beneath the weight of my indignation. I never believed anyone could talk to me like that. Unused to being contradicted, and even more so to being reprimanded by my subordinates, I feel myself shattering into a thousand pieces. Everyone understands how vulnerable I am, everyone knows I am extremely sensitive to comments which, when they are disobliging, make me so furious that I could drink the blood of him who is ill-mannered enough to make them.

Has Mansour taken leave of his senses?

I turn round and slump on the couch, with my head in my hands. Should I have Mansour shot on the spot? Should I kill him myself? A blast of white-hot emotion surges up in me.

'I'm not judging you, Rais—'

'Shut your mouth, you dog.'

He kneels in front of me. His voice suddenly calms down. He says in a conciliatory tone, 'All the silence on earth will not stop the truth coming out, Rais. I'm not blaming you, I'm telling you. I don't know if we will be alive tomorrow, Muammar my brother, my friend, my master. I could not care less about what happens to me or my family. I don't matter, I am completely insignificant. I'm afraid for you, not for anything else. If harm comes to you, Libya will never get over it. This beautiful country, which you have built by yourself against all the odds, will crumble like an old and rotten relic. They've already burnt your green flag, and replaced it with a flag of blood and mourning. Soon the national anthem you chose for us will be replaced by some comic-opera tune devoid of meaning. People are toppling your statues, defacing your portraits, looting your palaces. It's an apocalypse, Brotherly Guide. And I don't want to be part of it. Without you the boat will founder on unknown shores, its wreckage will be scattered across the waves, and there will be no trace left of what it once was. Without you the tribes will dig out their weapons that have lain dormant through centuries of bitterness, unsatisfied revenge and unpunished betrayals. There will be as many states as there are clans. The people you have joined together will rediscover their divisions, and this land you have constructed will turn into a dumping ground for every renunciation of revenge, a graveyard for every oath and prayer—'

'No more. Be quiet.'

Mansour weeps.

He grasps me by my wrists and clasps them to him as though he were taking hold of the destiny of all humanity.

'You must conquer this great misfortune, Rais. For the good of our homeland and for the stability of the region. I am ready to give my life, body and soul, for Libya to be returned to you.'

I push him away gently, carefully.

'Go, Mansour. Leave me alone now.'

When I look up, Mansour has gone – I think I must have fainted in the meantime.

8

I have been striding up and down the room, kicking out at thin air, only stopping to aim a deadly finger at a shadow or to wring an imaginary neck.

I am spitting with rage. That wimp Mansour dared to lay a hand on me. I have had family members executed for less. My gaols are heaving with undiplomatic, suspicious, restless and reckless people, people whose only crime was to be in the wrong place at the wrong time. I do not tolerate anyone discussing my orders, anyone questioning my judgements, anyone sulking in my presence. Everything I say is gospel, everything I think is a portent. He who does not listen to me is deaf, he who doubts me is damned. My anger is therapeutic for him who suffers it, my silence is self-discipline for him who reflects on it.

What did Mansour intend to achieve? Did he understand the extent of his folly? Blowing hot and cold like that, going off at tangents, jumping from allegiance to renunciation with disturbing ease.

He has badly unsettled me.

Libya would be a disaster without name or future if I were not here. This sacred land would be destined for misfortune and shame, our cemeteries would unleash their phantoms on our days and nights, and the living would turn into zombies, our stelae into gibbets!

I prowl around my cage, turning my shattered thoughts over and over in my mind, like a maniac driven by his obsessions. God alone is infallible! What was my Guard commander insinuating? That I am a troublemaker, or at fault? I have neither stirred up trouble nor fallen short, but have kept my promises in their entirety, won all my bets, risen to every challenge. The fury that now fills the streets with hate is a degeneration, an infamy, a sacrilege. An astounding ingratitude.

I am not a dictator.

I am the uncompromising sentinel, the she-wolf protecting her little ones, her fangs bigger than her jaws, the untamable jealous tiger that urinates on international conventions to mark his territory. I do not know how to bow and scrape or stare at the ground when a man looks down his nose at me. I walk with my head held high, with my full moon as my halo, and trample underfoot the masters of the world and their vassals.

People say I am a megalomaniac.

It is not true.

I am an exceptional being, providence incarnate, envied by the gods, able to make a faith of his cause.

Is it my fault that the valiant people of Libya, fallen so low, are compelled to ravage their homeland and make its blood run like filthy water, while the puppet masters rejoice at their martyrdom as they strip them of their last shred of dignity?

I lean my forehead against the wall, fingers linked behind my head, breathe in, breathe out. 'Go on, Muammar, aerate your soul, purge it of what is holding it back. Breathe gently, as if you were inhaling the scent of a woman, then expel the miasmas inside you … There, go on, good. Breathe, breathe. Imagine you are deep inside the Hanging Gardens, fill your lungs with the perfumes of Babylon. Let your spirit glide higher than the birds of paradise. You are Muammar Gaddafi, have you forgotten? Do not allow the small fry to pull you down from your cloud …'

My voice penetrates my senses, soothes me, purifies my being. The muffled pounding at my temples gradually starts to fade, my pulse becomes more regular. I feel much better.

I go back to the couch, pick up my Koran and open it at random. I cannot concentrate. Mansour's wailings return, pounding in my skull again like so many sledgehammers. I close my eyes to drive them out and cling to the summons of my soul.

It is the only Voice I know how to listen to: it calls me from the deepest depths of my being, makes my guts vibrate as a virtuoso does the strings of a lute. It is that Voice that incited me to overthrow a monarchy, to confront entire empires, to bring destiny to its knees. I have always known that I came into the world to mark it with my stamp, my way illuminated by that cosmic Voice that roars within me each time doubt appears, that proves to me every day that I am one of the blessed of heaven.

I have never listened to any other voice but my own.

My mother used to pull her hair out when she realised I was not listening to her, convinced that someone had put a spell on me. She took me to see all sorts of charlatans; their potions and charms did little to calm me down. I did just as I pleased, deaf to reproach, sealed off from everything that did not suit me. The chypsy has taken you, my mother sobbed, at the end of her tether. What have I done to you for you to make me ill from morning till night? Try to listen to reason, for once, just once … I did as she asked because I felt sorry for her, and a few hours later a neighbour came to the door of our house, shoving her snivelling kid in front of her as proof. You need to lock him up, your jinn, the neighbour would shout at my mother. Our kids can't go anywhere near him without him setting on them.

The truth was that I did not listen to anyone, so as not to have to hear their lies. People have always lied to me. Whenever I asked about my father my mother would answer quickly, 'He's in paradise.' I missed my father. Terribly. His not being there scarred me. I was jealous of the kids who scampered around their begetters. Even if they were not up to much, to me they looked as tall as gods. At the age of five I imagined what it would be like to take my own life. I wanted to die so that I could be with my father in heaven. Without him, existence had no flavour or attraction. So I chewed a poisonous herb, but all I got was a high fever and attacks of diarrhoea. When I was nine I went on and on at my uncle to make him tell me the truth about what had happened to my father. 'He was killed in a duel. To avenge the clan's honour.' I begged him to show me his grave. 'The brave do not really die. They are resurrected in their sons.' I refused to accept this far-fetched explanation. I became uncontrollable. The more my cousins stoked my unhappiness with their deadly insinuations, the worse my tantrums got. 'Your dad was expelled from the tribe. I heard he betrayed the tribe's trust …' A neighbour insisted that my father had simply been crushed by a tank during Rommel's great offensive. 'The poor man was out in a sandstorm with his goat. He didn't see the tank coming.' I was furious. 'Somebody must have collected his body.' – 'What could they have collected after his body was flattened by the tank's tracks? They couldn't even tell there was a goat there in the pulp they found.' I wept with disappointment, and when the neighbour started sniggering I pelted him furiously with rocks. I felt like burying the whole of humanity under heaps of stones.

My uncle no longer knew which saint to appeal to. He clapped his hands in impotence and apologised abjectly to the people who complained about my behaviour.

Until I was eleven years old, people treated me like a disturbed child. There was talk of confining me in the psychiatric clinic, but my parents were too poor. In the end, to restore some calm to the village, the clan all had to chip in to send me to school.

It was there, in front of a mirror in the school toilets, that the Voice started speaking to me. It assured me that my status as an orphan was nothing for me to be ashamed of, that the prophet Muhammad had not known his father, and nor had Isa Ibn Maryam.[7] It was a marvellous voice: it soaked up my pain like blotting paper. I spent most of my time just listening to it. Sometimes I went out into the desert on my own just to hear that voice and no other. I could talk to it without fear of being mocked by gossips. That was when I understood I was destined to become a legend.

At school in Sabha, then in Misrata, my classmates drank in my words to the point of intoxication. It was not me who bewitched them with my speeches, but the Voice that sang out through my being. My teachers

---

7 Jesus Christ in the Koran.

could not bear me. I defended the dunces, objected to the low marks they gave me, started strikes, cried foul, turned the poor kids against the well-off ones, openly criticised the king; none of the schools' suspensions and expulsions made any difference.

When I entered the Military Academy my vocation as a troublemaker only intensified. In spite of the regulations and charges. I quickly started to infiltrate various secret protest groups and began to dream of a great revolution that would elevate me to the level of a Mao or a Gamal Abdel Nasser.

'Brotherly Guide,' a voice calls from the other side of the door. 'The general requests you to join him. He is waiting for you downstairs.'

9

'The first section of the convoy has just arrived,' Abu-
Bakr announces as I come downstairs.

'How many vehicles?'

'Twelve. With fifty well-equipped troops.'

'What about my son?'

'He won't be long, according to Lieutenant-Colonel
Trid.'

At the mere mention of his name I feel myself
reviving.

'Is Trid here?'

'In the flesh, Brotherly Guide,' a voice to my left
thunders.

The lieutenant-colonel gives me a regulation salute.
I am so happy to see him that I feel like hugging him.
Brahim Trid is the youngest lieutenant-colonel in my
army. He is only thirty, but has countless acts of bravery
to his credit. Short, handsome, his moustache looking
almost out of place on his adolescent features, he
embodies the qualities I have wanted to instil in all my
officers. If I had a hundred men of his calibre, I could

outwit any army in the world. With his noble demeanour, uniform without a crease and freshly polished boots, he appears to float above the war and its chaos. The dust on his battledress sparkles like fairy dust. Intrepid, of extraordinary intelligence, Lieutenant-Colonel Brahim Trid is my own personal Otto Skorzeny. I have tasked him with several missions impossible and he has carried out every one of them with rare panache. It was Trid I entrusted with the training of the Azawad Malian dissidents, the recruitment of the Mauritanian revolutionaries, my destabilisation manoeuvres in the Sahel. With the evacuation of part of my family too, taking them to safety in Algeria. Not once has he let me down. His keenness, tenacity and valour set him apart from the officers of his generation. His mere presence among us is a relief. Even Mansour, to his surprise, is smiling.

'You were rumoured to be dead,' I tell him, careful not to let my pleasure show too much.

'Well, the rumours are mistaken,' he says, spreading his arms to show that he is fighting fit.

'How did you manage to find us?'

'He who loves will eventually find, Brotherly Guide. Your aura is my pole star.'

'Seriously.'

'The Benghazi rebels are so disorganised, any group could slip through without being discovered. I followed them to the city and sneaked between two roadblocks to get to District Two. Colonel Mutassim's men escorted me to point 36, and I made it the rest of the way with my eyes closed.'

'You have seen my son?'

'Yes, sir. He is doing a fantastic job. He has repelled an attack from the east and destroyed our munitions dumps. I left him regrouping. He supplied the eleven vehicles I've brought with me.'

'How is he?'

'Extremely well. He asked me to tell you that he will be an hour or two late, but that he has the situation in hand.'

He clears a table of the glasses standing on it, lays out a staff map and gives us his briefing.

'The situation is complicated but not insurmountable.'

He draws circles on the map with a coloured pencil to show our position and those of our enemies.

'The bulk of the rebel forces is stationed to the west. This sector is occupied by the Misrata militia. One section is advancing along the coast, the other is moving up from Sidi Be Rawaylah on the ring road in the direction of intersection 167. On that side everything's sealed by Al-Qaeda and the February 17th Martyrs Brigade … In the east the ungodly mob from Benghazi are advancing along the Abu Zahiyan road. The two groups are trying to join up at intersection 167 to isolate Bir Hamma.'

'Do they know our position?'

'I don't think so.'

'What is your plan?'

'We've got two options to try to break the blockade. The first is to punch through to the east. The dogs from Benghazi are more interested in destroying and looting than consolidating their front.'

'No,' the defence minister says, 'it's too risky that way.'

'Everything is risky, General, and everything is feasible.'

'Not when the rais is with us.'

The lieutenant-colonel acquiesces.

He moves on to his plan B.

'This afternoon a tactical withdrawal was observed along this thick line, which marks the rebels' initial front line. The enemy has pulled back by two or three kilometres towards the south-east and south-west, which leaves us a no man's land wide enough for us to move through as we wish. According to my reconnaissance units, the line from Bir Hamma to Khurb al-Aqwaz can be taken.'

'It may be an ambush,' Mansour objects. 'The gap is too obvious for it not to be a trap. If we let ourselves be drawn into a funnel, the enemy could take us in a pincer movement and destroy us. We wouldn't even be able to retreat if the Misrata militia has taken intersection 167.'

'We aren't facing a regular army,' the lieutenant-colonel insists. 'It's just a human flood overturning everything in its path. To the west the Islamists are going through the city with a fine-tooth comb. To the east, despite the anarchy in the Benghazi ranks, stragglers could intercept us all the way and we don't know the exact numbers of their forces. There are thousands of them roaming the streets looking for convoys to loot. The south is the only breakout route left to us.'

I approve of the lieutenant-colonel's choice – not because his arguments are irrefutable but because my intuition does not let me down. It was I who opted for the southerly withdrawal this morning. If I did not recall doing so earlier, it proves that it was the Voice who spoke for me. What I decide is what God wants. Did I not escape the bombing that targeted my residence at Bab al-Azizia the night I was celebrating my beloved grandson's birthday with my whole family, a raid that cost the lives of my sixth son Saif al-Arab and his three sons? I emerged from the debris without a scratch. The perils I have faced during my reign, the non-stop plots and assassination attempts, would have got the better of anyone else. God watches over me. I do not doubt it for a second. In a few hours the blockade will open before me like the Red Sea before Moses. I shall pierce the enemy lines as easily as a needle pierces cloth.

'All we have to do is wait for Mutassim,' I conclude.

'As soon as he comes, we shall withdraw.'

'Four o'clock is the most favourable time,' the general ventures.

'Out of the question,' I interrupt him. 'There is no favourable time, Abu-Bakr. We need to get out of this wasps' nest as soon as possible. The coalition's warplanes will be dropping their bombs on us at any moment.'

'I agree,' Mansour says.

'It makes no difference whether you agree or not,' I shout at him. 'I am in command here. Prepare to withdraw. Mutassim will not need to leave his vehicle. As soon as his convoy approaches, we form up in column formation and we head out. I do not want anyone to know that I am with my troops.'

The lieutenant-colonel picks up his map, folds it carefully and replaces it in his briefcase.

'You may go now, Colonel Trid. You need to get your breath back. You are a remarkable officer,' I add, glancing scornfully at the general and Guard commander. 'You deserve my respect.'

The young officer does not turn away. With a mischievous smile he says to me, 'I didn't come empty-handed, Brotherly Guide.'

He snaps his fingers. Two soldiers push a bound prisoner into the room. He is wearing a flapping pair of jogging pants torn at the knees and a nondescript sweater. His complexion is greyish-brown, he has the physique of a flabby bear, and his face bears the marks of a beating. His eye, ringed with a thick purplish bruise, is swollen and horribly closed. His white hair and jowls put him in his fifties.

They throw him at my feet. He falls to his knees and I see a deep gash bleeding on the back of his neck.

'Who is he?'

'Captain Jaroud, General Younis's aide-de-camp,' Trid says, proud of his trophy.

'Is he not a little old for the job?'

'Correct. This coward was a corporal, then staff sergeant and the general's personal driver. He was promoted to officer rank by Younis without attending a military academy.'

I push the prisoner away with my foot. He stinks so badly that I hold my nose.

'Did you find him in a drain?'

'I picked him up hitchhiking on the ring road,' the lieutenant-colonel says ironically.

'I was trying to find you, sir,' the prisoner moans. 'I swear.'

I look at him in disgust.

'Because General Younis had dismissed you?'

'I'm not important enough for anyone to be that interested in me, sir.'

'Why did he betray me?'

'I don't know, sir.'

'He thought he saw an opportunity to get in with the rebels and save his career,' Mansour says.

'His ambitions were outrageous,' the minister adds.

I prod the former aide-de-camp once again.

'Have you swallowed your tongue?'

A guard hits him hard on the back of the neck.

'Answer the rais.'

The prisoner gulps several times before quavering, 'General Younis was jealous, sir. He didn't like you. Once I surprised him in his office with his arm outstretched and a revolver pointed at your picture.'

'And you kept it to yourself.'

He bows his head. His shoulders heave with the pressure of a muffled sob.

'You could have warned me.'

'The general must have dangled the prospect of greater status in front of him,' the lieutenant-colonel remarks.

Mansour gives him a look that warns him not to intervene.

The renegade sniffs, wipes his nose on his shoulder. He does not have the strength to raise his gaze to my face. The same guard jabs him with the barrel of his rifle.

'The rais asked you a question.'

'I was scared of him …' the prisoner admits. 'To be

aide-de-camp to a vulture like him is like expecting to be devoured raw at any moment. He could sense things that were happening miles away and he read people's minds like a book. If he had the slightest suspicion he reacted instantly. And he was ruthless. I felt in danger every time he looked at me. The only way I could function with him was by taking antidepressants.'

'How did he die?'

'Like a dog, sir.'

'How do dogs die?' the minister of defence asks. 'I had one once. He died of old age, surrounded by my sons' affection. Is that how General Younis ended up?'

'Was he really killed, or was it a cover-up? He was invited to the Élysée palace by Nicolas Sarkozy, after all. That is a big deal. Younis is an impressive negotiator. I feel sure he saved his skin. Perhaps as we speak he is in some tax haven somewhere, making the most of his fortune?'

'He was executed, sir. There's no doubt about it.'

'Were you there?'

'No, sir.'

'So how can you be so categorical? People deluge us with inventions these days. I have even heard people say it was me who was behind the general's assassination. I would have been delighted for that to be the case, except that it is not true.'

'He wasn't there, but he knows something about

it,' the lieutenant-colonel informs me, despite being reprimanded by Mansour. He crouches next to the traitor, grabs his ear and forces him to raise his head. 'Tell the rais what happened, you son of a rat. You were at your boss's side when he was summoned to that sham trial. Tell him what you saw and heard that day, nothing more.'

'I'm thirsty,' the turncoat groans.

The minister sends for someone to bring water.

Having quenched his thirst, the prisoner tells the story without stopping. According to him, General Abdul Fatah Younis had observed the balance of power beginning to shift dangerously towards the faction of the February 17th Martyrs Brigade commanded by the Islamist Abdelhakim Belhadj, a hardline activist who had spent six years locked up in my gaols. Despite the enormous support the general had brought to the rebellion, his operational powers were being whittled away. Relegated to the position of a mere adviser to the National Transitional Council, he felt that the hothouse atmosphere was rapidly becoming stifling and that he needed to take charge of things again, but they had only left him his eyes to weep with. The French did not like him; they had used him as a common pawn in their negotiations and were ready to drop him now that he had no more than a walk-on part and no influence on events. As for the Americans, his fate was sealed: the general was, at worst, a dead man walking, at best a war criminal to be packed up and delivered to the good offices of the International Criminal Court.

'Keep it short,' Mansour orders him. 'Just tell us how your boss died.'

'I'm coming to that, sir.'

'We're not here to wait for you, scum. Stick to the facts.'

The traitor clears the frog from his throat and says, 'The general was accused of being a double agent, of working for you, Rais, and for Sarkozy. I was with him when he was served with the arrest warrant, signed by Abdul Jalil in person.[8] He was spitting with rage, shouting that he had been betrayed. I escorted him to the military tribunal where the charges against him were read out. The general protested, then said that he did not recognise the court's legitimacy and attempted to return to his headquarters. A cousin of mine, who had joined the Islamists and was at the tribunal, stopped me from going with the general. He advised me to go to our aunt's house in Tripoli and not to show myself on the street. The general was held by the Islamists as he left the tribunal and driven away in a 4×4. He was executed the same day.'

'How?'

'My cousin came to our aunt's house in Tripoli

---

8 Mustafa Abdul Jalil, chairman of the National Transitional Council (NTC).

afterwards. He had been one of the abductors. He told me that the general had tried to jump out of the 4×4. They knocked him out and took him to a shed to be interrogated. He was tortured with pliers and a blowlamp. They cut off his toes, put one of his eyes out and cut his stomach open with a hacksaw.'

'Your cousin's seen too many slasher movies,' Mansour says sceptically.

'He recorded it on his mobile and he showed me how the general was killed. I spent three days throwing up and three nights screaming in my sleep. I'm still shaking ...' Suddenly raising his head, he goes on, white-faced, 'These people aren't human, Rais. Just coming across them in the street gave me the shivers. They call themselves Muslims but they hardly leave any work for the Devil to do. They kill kids as if they were squashing flies. I've never seen anything more horrible than their expression. It's like they're looking at you with the eyes of death itself. When my cousin suggested I join his squad, I said yes on the spot. He'd have slashed my belly open, like the general, in front of our aunt and without a qualm, if I'd hesitated for a second. But I couldn't live with those barbarians. I was scared to death just at the thought of sitting down to a meal with them. That night, after my cousin had gone to sleep, I ran away without looking back, as fast as my legs could carry me. I intended to get back to Sirte to rejoin your troops, Rais, but the town was swarming with rebels who were shooting up anything that moved. I wandered for days and nights, hiding in cellars. When I recognised the lieutenant-colonel on the ring road, it felt like I was waking up from a nightmare.'

'Don't worry, you're still in it,' the lieutenant-colonel promises him.

'Rais,' the prisoner begs, raising himself on his knees, 'I didn't betray you. From the beginning my only thought was to rejoin your forces. It's the truth, I swear it.'

'There's no such thing. People believe what suits them, and your story doesn't suit me.'

He crawls after me.

'I worship you more than my father and my ancestors, Brotherly Guide. I've got four kids and a wife who's half mad. Spare me, for the love of the prophet. I want to take my place among your soldiers again. I'll show myself worthy of your trust—'

Trust?

That old chestnut!

I banned that poisonous word from my vocabulary before I learnt to walk. Trust is a little death. I had to be wary of everything and everyone, especially the most loyal of my loyalists, because they are the ones best informed about my faults. To guarantee my own longevity I did not confine myself to listening in on people's thoughts or bribing their consciences – I was ready to execute my twin to keep my siblings at arm's length.

And yet, despite the draconian measures I took, the elaborate precautions and the purges, I have been betrayed. By the most loyal of my loyalists. General Younis, whom I considered my partner in crime, whom I loved more than a brother, the man who boasted of being godfather to my son, who never forgot me in his prayers and took my lapses to be coded signs: he betrayed me. How can I not view his tragic end as a divine punishment? By rejecting my blessing, he signed his own death warrant. I do not even feel contempt for him, just a vague sadness, a kind of pity made of elusive ingredients, which simultaneously calms and comforts me.

'I beg you, Rais,' the renegade sobs, 'I tried to rejoin your forces; I swear it on the head of what is most precious to me in this world.'

'The only precious thing left to you in this world is your head, and it is not worth a radish,' I tell him.

I turn to the two soldiers.

'Send him straight to hell.'

The traitor attempts to resist the arms restraining him, he writhes and struggles, his face contorted. They drag him without ceremony into the courtyard. I hear him begging me and weeping. His lamenting turns to shrieks of terror as he disappears into the night, then, having exhausted every appeal, he starts to blaspheme.

'You're nothing but a madman, Muammar, a raving bloodthirsty madman. Cursed be the womb that bore you and the day you came into this world ... You're nothing but a bastard, Muammar, a bastard ...'

Someone must have knocked him out then, because he suddenly stopped.

In the silence that follows, the word 'bastard' goes on ringing in my ear in a chorus of heart-rending echoes so monstrous that my cosmic Voice, which has always known how to speak to me in my moments of solitude, has curled up into itself like a frightened snail.

Around me, Mansour, the minister and the lieutenant-colonel look down, their heads bowed, paralysed by the obscene insults proffered by the supplicant.

I go back up to my room to recover from the affront.

10

Bastard, bastard, bastard ...

The insult ricochets around the walls, pierces me from all sides, making a million toxins explode under my skin. At every bang that rings out from the town, at every door that shuts downstairs, at every object that falls on the floor, I hear bastard. If I filled my ears with concrete or burst my eardrums, I would still hear it above the noise of the war that is raging in my country.

Yet it has always been there, that degrading word, waiting to ambush me on sleepless nights and pin me to my pillows. Whenever the roistering died down and the shutters closed on my private moments, whenever my concubines, drunk on my seed, drifted into sleep, whenever van Gogh retreated into his canvas and silence merged with darkness in my palace, that word kept me company beneath the sheets and stopped me sleeping, sometimes until morning.

It is a word with a history that has ruined mine.

I had just heard about my promotion to captain. That evening, outstretched on my bed, I could not decide whether to celebrate my new rank at home, with my wife and a few friends, or in Fezzan, among my tribe. In my sleep van Gogh appeared to me as a knight in armour, trapped at the bottom of a frozen lake … In the morning, a jeep stopped me outside my building. The driver, a young red-headed NCO in a scruffy uniform, told me he had been ordered to drive me to HQ. I thought I was being summoned to a ceremony or to some honour of that sort and climbed up next to the driver, smoothing my tunic and straightening my cap.

At HQ they directed me to Block B, a sinister-looking building belonging to His Majesty King Idris as-Senussi's special services. Never having hidden my desire to be appointed to an embassy in a land of plenty somewhere, I climbed the stairs to the third floor with high hopes – so high, I nearly caught my foot in the carpet and went flying.

A corporal greeted me like a dog at a bowling alley. His disdain corresponded to the attitude I thought every flunkey in a repressive system had to have; I did not attach any importance to it. I was led into a waiting room, austerely furnished with a pedestal table and a row of iron chairs whose paint was flaking off. I waited there, getting more and more bored, for three hours without anyone coming to see if I was still there or even still in this world. By the time the corporal reappeared I was on the point of losing my temper completely.

Major Jalal Snoussi was waiting for me in his office. He was a pockmarked, red-faced officer with a wisp of hair and grotesque ears. His hog-like features pointed to the insatiable glutton concealed beneath his uniform, but his expression would have silenced the blackest of sheep with a glance. In my eyes he represented everything I deplored in an officer: pot-bellied, crude, traducing the essence of the martial calling that his tunic was supposed to confer on him.

There was no love lost between us. I had known him since the Academy, where I had had him as an instructor during my second year as an officer cadet. He taught topography, but was incapable of finding his way with a map and a compass. His real task at the Academy consisted in identifying the bad apples among the cadets and writing daily reports on the acts and movements of new recruits: he was the army's official informer.

It did not surprise me in the least to find him in an office on the third floor of Block B, except that I understood immediately that my dream of a foreign posting was not on the agenda.

The major did not offer me a chair. He hitched up his belly to sit down, leafed disdainfully through a few papers that made up my file, then, after rubbing his nose, stared intensely at me.

'Do you know why I have summoned you, Lieutenant?'

'Captain,' I reminded him.

'Not yet. Your promotion will only take effect two months from now, which gives me the opportunity to oppose it.'

'You would oppose a decree, Major?'

'Absolutely. It's one of my prerogatives. His Majesty's special services have the right to annul any decision up to the highest level if it puts the kingdom in danger.'

He was exaggerating. He was just an underling mouldering in a cupboard through which soldiers who had come from the people had to pass in order to be intimidated; a bootlicker, happy to be trodden on like bird shit whenever he was faced with those stronger than him but ready to send an innocent man to the gallows to show his master how good he was at keeping an eye on things.

Because his name sounded like the king's, Major Jalal Snoussi liked people to think that he was also from Algeria, as was His Majesty, and that he had excellent relations with the crown prince.

In reality he was as noble as a worm-infested jackal. He had a finger in every rotten pie, his eyes were always bigger than his stomach, and he demanded that his palm be greased for the slightest of favours. He filled his belly at the monarch's expense, never putting his hand in his own pocket, and replenishing his supplies at every garrison where he had the chefs at his mercy: every night he took delivery of enough to feed a family for a month – poultry, a whole sheep, skinned and jointed by a master butcher, crates of fruit and vegetables, cases of tinned food – and every morning the ravenous waifs would fight like hell around his bins, which army wits had dubbed 'the canteen of miracles'.

I loathed him and he knew it.

'You're here because that tentacle in your mouth is so long we could hang you with it,' he shouted, slapping the file down on his desk.

I did not react. If this fat pig had any evidence against me, he would have sent me straight to the firing squad. I was convinced he was making it up.

'I've got my eye on you, Muammar.'

'Which one, Major? The one that squints or the one that swivels from side to side?'

'Both of them, Lieutenant. The ones that will end up sending you six feet under. I know about your little schemes, you fucking devil. You fill the heads of cretins with your pathetic revolutionary theories, and you dare speak ill of the monarchy that has seen fit to make an officer out of the snivelling beggar you once were. You still stink of the shit of your camels, you know that?'

'The important thing is not where one comes from, but the road one has taken. No one has ever done me any favours. I have studied without a single grant and I have made myself who I am. Your rank does not give you permission to insult me, Major.'

'It gives me permission to walk all over you. In your

shoes I would not play the hero. You're not cut out for it. A bigmouth is all you are. A fine talker who believes in his own wild imaginings. I've been told about the secret meetings you have been holding all over the shop. You're whipping up a band of hot-headed fools in your unit. Try and deny it.'

'I challenge you to produce the proof, Major. Your accusation is extremely serious. I am a competent officer of integrity. I carry out my work according to regulations and I know my rights. I do not steal my men's rations and I do not ask for a dirham from anyone I do a favour for.'

He looked as if he was about to burst into flames, and nearly ripped the papers in his hands to shreds.

'Exactly what are you insinuating, Lieutenant?'

'I am not insinuating anything, I am being perfectly clear and I am ready to defend my words in front of a tribunal. Are you ready to do the same?'

'No, no, go back to what you just said. What is this tale of rations and dirhams?'

'Do you want me to draw you a picture, Major? Everyone knows about your trafficking. As for whoever has put you up to this, I do not know what he seeks to gain from it, but I shall not let myself be walked all over. I have done nothing wrong, and your allegations are as far-fetched as they are dangerous. Do you realise what you are suggesting? That I am an agitator?'

I was shouting now, to unnerve him.

He asked me to calm down and have a chair. I refused and remained standing, trembling with anger. There was very little in the file that was burning his fingers and was probably not even mine.

He mopped his face with a handkerchief, breathing heavily.

I had him.

'I want your informer's name. He will answer for his calumnies in front of a court martial.'

'That's enough,' the major said. 'Be quiet. I summoned you because I have your best interests at heart. I hear word that you're indulging in reactionary statements ...'

'"I hear word". Who from?'

'I'm doing my job, like you. I am not allowed to leave anything to chance. I've heard that—'

'That what?'

The major really lost it then.

To shut him up, I clicked my heels and left his office, promising loudly that I would take the whole story to the head of the service prosecuting authority. The truth was that I was so scared, I was doing everything I could to confuse him. The next thing I knew was a sergeant stopping me in the corridor.

'Muammar Gaddafi, come into my office.'

He had not saluted; he stood in front of me with his jacket over his belt and his sleeves rolled up, which was against regulations. For someone like me, a stickler for discipline, the NCO's provocatively careless turnout bordered on sacrilege. And not only had he addressed me by name without using my rank, he had practically ordered me to follow him to his office. I could hardly contain my fury.

Slim and blond, the sergeant had the look of the élite, blue eyes and a girlish mouth, one of those cosseted young go-getters from the old Libyan bourgeoisie employed in His Majesty's special services so that they learnt how to trample ordinary people underfoot. I had met dozens of them at the lycée, where I had had to put up with their overblown arrogance, which was so inflated I felt like killing every one of them. The deep hatred I felt towards these golden boys had been the seed of my diatribes. Every time I came across one of them, I spat secretly to ward off evil spells.

The sergeant was only interested in a single detail.

'There is a minor problem with your filiation, Muammar.'

'What problem? And say "lieutenant" when you address me. We did not grow up herding goats together.'

'I have never herded goats, I'm glad to say,' he retorted sourly, with heavy emphasis. 'I don't need to remind you that function trumps rank, Lieutenant. In this office it is I who decide what happens, like it or not. My department has ordered me to verify the information on your identification form. You will be aware that the higher you rise in rank, the more important the duties you will be called on to fulfil. In consequence it becomes imperative not to make an error about the applicant ...'

'And the problem is?'

'Your father ...'

Already outraged at being pushed around by this little NCO, I was doubly outraged to have to answer to him about my family.

'He died honourably.'

'That is not what I have on your form. According to the inquiry we have carried out in your clan, you are the son of an unknown father. Certain loose talk suggests that you are the natural child of a Corsican by the name of Albert Preziosi, a pilot rescued and nursed in your tribe after his plane was shot down by a German fighter in 1941.'

My fist had a mind of its own. The sergeant got it full in the face and fell backwards, his nose broken. I did not have a chance to finish him. Four men leapt on me and threw me on the floor. Major Jalal Snoussi stood sniggering in the doorway, his arms folded. He was in heaven, delighted at having outwitted me. I had fallen into his trap. The summons to his office had been merely the first stage of his plan, which had been to make me lose my composure, so that I would react as I had done to his subordinate's provocation.

'What did I say to you, Bedouin? That I will oppose

your promotion. Do you believe me now?'

I had thought that he was just a zealous penpusher with a lot of lard where his brain should be. But the major could have shown the Devil a trick or two.[9]

I was brought before a disciplinary hearing. After a period of close arrest and the deferment of my promotion to captain, I travelled home to Fezzan to settle an old score with my clan.

Hostile and harsh, Fezzan is a version of hell which, because there was nowhere better or because they were damned, the Ghous had claimed for themselves the way a starving hyena claims a leftover piece of rotting carcass. There was a time when I took it for hell itself.

Ground down by thirst and dizzying heat, Fezzan was like me. I was as naked and empty as the desert expanding the circle of its desolation.

Sitting under an acacia, I daydreamed about nomads, brigands, pilgrims, deserters, caravan drivers, adventurers, travellers who had lost their way, lords and servants who had paused under this tree, bristling with thorns, wondering what roads they had taken after their

---

9 During the clean-up operation, which I took personal charge of, to disinfect the republic's institutions of the monarchist vermin, I forced Major Jalal Snoussi to dig his own grave with his bare hands.

rest and whether they had arrived at their destination.

I was more unhappy than it is normally possible to be, as miserable as the skeletal shadow of the acacia brushing away the sand, as frantic as the wild, spindly roots tangled around me, not knowing where to bury their sorrow.

The furnace around me was nothing to the furnace that was burning my soul.

What had I come to find in the desert? The retreat of silence or the agony of time passing? There was nothing for me here. My points of reference had as much solidity as the mirages shimmering deceptively in the distance. Had I come to listen to the Voice, or to erase the sergeant's voice? Neither seemed capable of reaching me in the tumult of my frustration. Like a tightrope walker I wobbled in the void, sure that flying away would be as tragic for me as falling.

I sat moping all day under the acacia tree, where my uncle, tired of waiting for me, eventually came to find me.

He said, 'Why are you sitting here, Muammar?'

'Where else should I go?'

'Come home. You've been roasting in the sun for hours. It's not good for you. You'll get sunstroke.'

'Is that all?'

'Is it true what they're saying, that you've been dismissed from the army?'

'They have suspended me.'

'How is it possible?'

'I punched an officer.'

'You punched an officer?'

'I would have punched the king himself.'

'What has got into you, my son?'

'I am not anyone's son.'

I faced him.

With his spine stooped under the burden of his years and his face like a halo of dust, my uncle looked like a cloth stuck on a pole. Poverty had sucked him dry, leaving him just his old hands to reflect his fate.

I challenged him.

'Who is Albert Preziosi?'

He put a finger to his cheek, eyelashes lowered, and thought for a long time.

'Is it a name from among us?'

'It is a Christian name.'

'I have never known a Christian in my life.'

'Try and remember. It goes back a long way, to a time when the Christians used to turn up in our houses uninvited.'

'The colonists preferred to be near the sea. The desert was not for them.'

I got to my feet, towering over him by a full head. He looked smaller than a gnome.

'Are you telling me that not a single infidel soldier ever ventured into our territory? There are places here that still bear the traces of the Afrika Korps's Panzers. Relics of tanks less than three kilometres from this spot. By the 1940s you were already a father. You must have come across a Christian or two. A deserter or a wounded man whom the clan looked after, out of Muslim charity.'

He shook his head, his brow furrowed.

'You do not remember a plane shot down in a dogfight that crashed near here in 1941?'

He shook his head again.

'The pilot was not killed. Our people went to his aid and hid him and nursed him ... It is impossible that you can have forgotten an event of that kind. He was a Frenchman, a Corsican ...'

'No plane came down here. Not during the war, or before or after.'

'Look at me!'

He stood in front of me, shaking his chin from left to right.

My voice snapped like an explosion.

'Is it true that I am a bastard, the piss of some dog of a Corsican who passed through here?'

The crudity of my speech made him flinch. It is not in our upbringing to utter obscenities in front of those who are older than us. But he did not protest. He saw how angry I was and did not feel capable of confronting it. What he said next, in a whisper, he did not mean to say.

'I don't see what you mean.'

'Do you ever see anything apart from the end of your nose? Go on, tell me the truth. Is it true that I am the runt of some dog of a Corsican?'

'Who has said such an outrageous thing to you?'

'That is not an answer.'

'Your father died in a duel. I've told you a thousand times.'

'In that case, where is his tomb? Why is his body not in our cemetery with the rest of our departed?'

'I—'

'Be quiet. You are nothing but a liar. You have all lied to me. I have no reason to be grateful to you in the slightest. If my father is still in this world I shall find him, even if I have to turn over every stone on earth. If he is dead I shall find his tomb eventually. As for all of you, I banish you from my heart and I will spend the rest of my days cursing you until the good Lord cries out, "Enough!"'

I never spoke another word to my uncle.

After I had overthrown the king and proclaimed the republic, I went back, my head still ringing with the crowd's acclamation, to celebrate my revolution in my tribe. I was coming back to take my revenge on my clan. They had kept a secret from me, and I had proved that I could survive it. Fezzan changed its look for me that morning. The desert was offering its nakedness to me as a blank page, ready to receive the epic of my unstoppable rise.

Sitting cross-legged in the *kheïma* of the most senior elder, my smile wider than the crescent on the top of a minaret, I relished the rapture I aroused among my people. They no longer looked down on me, they were prostrating themselves at my feet. The kids were running all over the place, overexcited by my presence; the women spied on me from the depths of their hiding places; the men pinched themselves until they drew blood. In my tailored uniform, like a prince in his state regalia, I had drunk tea with my nearest relations and a few comrades. The desert rang with our bursts of laughter. A full moon graced the sky, heated white-hot. In the middle of the day. My uncle stood outside the tent, not knowing if he should rejoice at my return or feel its pain. I had not acknowledged him. It was no longer very important to me to know if I was a Corsican's bastard or a brave man's son.

I was my own offspring.

My own begetter.

Are we all our fathers' children? Was Isa Ibn Maryam the son of God, or the child of a rape that went unacknowledged, or just the result of a rash flirtation? What does it matter? Jesus knew how to fashion his short young life into immortality, to turn his Calvary into a

Milky Way and his name into the password for paradise. What counts is what we succeed in leaving behind us. How many world-class conquerors have fathered good-for-nothing kings? How many civilisations have disappeared the moment they were handed on to heirs of insufficient calibre? How many shackled slaves have broken their chains to build colossal empires? I had no need to know who my father had been, or to look for the grave of an illustrious stranger. I was Muammar Gaddafi. For me the Big Bang had taken place the morning I took over the radio station in Benghazi to announce to a drowsing populace that I was their saviour and their redemption. Bastard or orphan, I had transformed myself into a nation's destiny by becoming its legitimate path and identity. For having given birth to a new reality, I no longer had anything to envy the gods of mythology or the heroes of history.

I was worthy of being only Myself.

11

I am reading the Koran, shut away in my room, when the air strike hits District Two, one missile, then another … The third is so powerful that the last panes are blasted out of the windows and hit the floor in a chilling shattering of glass.

The awaited coalition attack has begun.

I go out into the corridor. On the ground floor I hear someone shouting orders to switch off all the lights and not to go out into the courtyard. The few candles lighting the living room downstairs are quickly put out. A fourth missile hits, not far from our school headquarters. A sort of feverishness takes hold of me, making me excited and curious. I want to be present at the bombardment of my city, and I take the stairs that lead to the terrace four at a time.

I expected something climactic, a sky slashed by shooting stars, adorned with balls of fire the size of exploding suns, with searchlights aimed in the direction of the attack, soldiers returning fire, fire engines tearing to where the missiles have hit and burning winds starting up on every side – but all I get is a low-grade performance as miserable as it is amateurish, seeing only a city without courage exposed to the fury of the drones, inert in its dust and dirt like a tart in her filthy sheets. Apart from the bombs raining down from an indifferent sky and the targets smoking like shreds of rags carried away on the wind, Sirte is as depressing as one of History's rejects. Not a single pair of headlights, not one alarm wailing, not a shot fired from a rooftop: nothing but the crump of explosions and a darkness filled with poltergeists who have suddenly gone to ground, their fingers to their lips so they do not give themselves away.

I am disappointed.

I remember the night of Friday 28 March 2003, when a rain of fire deluged Baghdad. I was pinned to my armchair at Bab al-Azizia, in front of my plasma screen, completely transfixed by the blue-green darkness saturating the city of Harun al-Rashid. The flares swelled in the middle of the Tomahawk ballet, the anti-aircraft machine guns traced exciting phosphorescent lines of dots in the sky, buildings collapsed in a tumult of concrete and steel, ammunition dumps burst in great arrays of sizzling comets. It was a magical sight, a terrible wonderland. The coalition's apocalyptic firework display came up against the Iraqis' valour. David and Goliath were waging a titanic battle in a performance designed by a choreographer of genius. The air-raid sirens merged with the ambulance sirens to make a symphony of misfortune that was unbearable in its intensity and beauty. I could have died that night in Baghdad's wounded arms, at the heart of a proud nation so admirable in its fighting spirit; I would have liked to die pinned to a column that shattered into a thousand pieces, or be blown apart by a shell, shouting, 'Death to the invader.' Nothing can be more gratifying for a martyr than to give up his soul without surrendering, identifying himself with every fireball, every rattling breech, every piece of flesh caught in the coil of the supreme sacrifice.

What a disappointment not to see any of that in my own country.

Sirte is the pits, an old, rotting rug being beaten to pieces, a doormat to wipe your filthy boots on. It looks like the kind of place the gods chose to mourn their Olympus.

'Don't stay out there, Brotherly Guide.'

Abu-Bakr begs me to take cover. He stands at the top of the stairs, too frightened to join me on the terrace. His pallor gleams in the half-light, like a candle in a death chamber.

'Brotherly Guide, please, this way.'

I feel like spitting at him.

Mansour and Lieutenant-Colonel Trid come running.

'Please, Rais, don't stay there.'

'Why not?' I say. 'It is my city they are destroying. How can I look elsewhere, or cover my face?'

Abu-Bakr ventures out onto the terrace.

'Go back to your hole,' I order him. 'I am not like Ben Ali, ready to sneak away. I was born in this land and this land will be my tomb.'

'You could be injured.'

'What about it?'

'We need you, Rais.'

'Go. That is an order. I am not afraid of dying.'

A missile hits a few blocks away from the school. The defence minister retreats to the top of the stairs, his hands covering his ears, bent double. Mansour throws himself down. Only the lieutenant-colonel dares to come towards me, not knowing how to convince me to follow him.

The building that has been hit turns into a gigantic torch. The trees around it catch fire in turn, casting an unearthly light on the street, strewn with white-hot rubble.

Intoxicated by the noise of weapons and the folly of men, I find myself yelling, my arms out wide, calling down the heaven's thunder.

'You will not take me alive. I am not a clove of garlic to be strung up on a rope. I will fight to the last drop of my blood ... Come and get me, you dogs! I am a soldier of Allah; death is my mission. My place is in paradise, at the side of the prophets, surrounded by angels and houris, and my earthly tomb will carry as many crowns as a meadow has flowers ... What did you think? That I would hide down a well until someone came to flush me out? You will not swab my cheek with your cotton swabs. You will not expose me on prime-time TV with a tramp's beard. And you, Sarkozy, you will not have the honour of flying my scalp on the roof of your National Assembly.'

'I beg you, Rais, come with me,' Trid pleads with me. I am not listening to him.

I hear only my own piercing cries, ringing out over the chaos of the explosions. I am a roaring inferno. A supernatural force has taken hold of me. I feel capable of confronting hurricanes.

A bomb explodes close to the school. Its shock wave stings my face, whipping up my anger. I climb up onto the parapet, open my arms wide, my chest thrust out, my chin forward.

The lieutenant-colonel grips my waist to stop me stepping up onto the wall's outer ledge. He suspects that I am about to throw myself off. I push him away with a hand, turn back to the massacre and go on with my railing against the entire world.

'Look! I'm up here, flesh and blood, on my pedestal. Must I sacrifice myself before you see me? Come on, show some guts, you cowards; come and get me if you're man enough. You'll find that I'm not Ben Ali, or Saddam or Bin Laden.'

'Rais, there'll be snipers across the street.'

'Then let them show themselves. They couldn't hit a mountain, they're shaking with fear.'

The lieutenant-colonel wraps his arms around my waist again. It is as if his embrace is pressing on my rage to squirt it up to the stars. I lean on him for support, put my hands around my mouth like a megaphone and hurl my cries further than an artillery shell.

'Curses be upon you, Saddam Hussein! Why did you let yourself be taken alive and executed on the first day of Eid? You could have put a bullet in your brain and robbed the Crusaders of the pleasure of their ghoulish revenge. Because of you, the prophet Muhammad and his people do not dare raise their eyes to God any longer ... But I shall stand straight before the Lord. I shall look him in the eye till He turns away. Because He wouldn't trouble himself to unleash the Ababil on these infidels who heap calumnies and defecate without restraint upon a Muslim land.'[10]

My shouts pour out into space like a raging torrent of the elements; the sky and earth intermingle, then the abyss ...

---

10 In the Koran the Ababil were a race of birds that saved Mecca from the Yemeni army by dropping clay bricks on its elephants as they approached.

12

I am cold.

In the cavern in which I find myself it is as black as if no light had shone there since the beginning of time. I grope my way, fear clawing at my stomach; I have no idea where I am going, but I know that I am not alone. An intangible presence is hovering around me. I hear the sound of footsteps. When I stop, the sound stops too.

'Who is there?'

Silence.

'Who is there? I am not deaf. Play hide-and-seek as much as you like, I can hear you.'

'All you can hear is the echo of your own fear, Muammar.'

I turn towards the Voice; it rings through the cavern, ricocheting off the stone, washing over me and dying away in a yawning sigh.

'I am not afraid.'

'Yes you are.'

'Who should I be afraid of? I am the dauntless Guide, and I walk with my head held so high that the very stars draw back from me.'

'In that case, why do you retreat in the darkness?'

'Perhaps I am dead.'

'Having skipped your punishment? Too easy, don't you think?'

'Who are you? Angel or devil?'

'Both. I was even God, once.'

'Then show yourself, if you are brave enough.'

Something moves in the depth of the cavern and comes closer. I can just make out a human form. It is a wretch dressed in rags, with a shaggy tangled beard and an endless rope tied around his neck that he drags with him, among his chains.

'Who are you?'

'Don't you recognise me? No more than a minute ago you were heaping curses on me.'

'Saddam Hussein?'

'Or what is left of him: a poor devil wandering in the darkness.'

'Then I am dead.'

'Not yet. For your soul to rest, it must first make sure it undergoes the suffering of your flesh.'

'What do you want from me?'

'To look you in the face and read the terror that's written there now. You've insulted me, cursed me and spat on me. Let me remind you that I was hanged by America and its allies, but you will be lynched by your own people.'

'Your people betrayed you too.'

'It's not the same, Muammar. Under my reign Iraq was a great nation. Harun al-Rashid was no greater a ruler than I was. My universities produced geniuses. Every night Baghdad made merry, every seed I sowed sprouted before it touched the ground. But you, Muammar, what did you turn your people into? A starving mob who'll devour you whole.'

'I can't know your fate, Hussein. But my destiny is in my hands. And God's too.'

'God is with no one. Didn't He let His own son die on the cross? He won't come to your aid. He'll watch you die like a dog under a hail of stones. And when your soul departs your body He won't even be there to meet it. You'll wander in the darkness, as I do, until you become no more than a shadow among the shadows.'

'Perhaps, but I am not dead yet. I have the strength to fight and to turn the situation to my advantage. I shall not end up like you. My throne is summoning me back, and in less than a week people will be celebrating my victory and no one will ever raise their voice against me again.'

'No one celebrates the wind. Wherever it shows itself, all it does is pass by. What it takes with it is of little importance, and what it leaves behind will be erased by time.'

'I am not the wind. I am Muammar Gaddafi!'

My shout awakens me. The ceiling spins in slow motion; my senses slowly return. I am lying stretched out on the couch in my bedroom, feeling woozy, exhausted, my throat raw. A small table has been placed next to me with a tray on which there is a cold meal: an egg sandwich, a chocolate bar, some jam and a carafe of water.

'You must get your strength back, Rais,' Abu-Bakr tells me. 'The doctor has diagnosed mild hypoglycaemia. You haven't eaten anything since yesterday lunchtime.'

'What happened to me?'

'A mild attack of exhaustion. Nothing serious. Eat, please. It will do you good.'

Around me, in addition to the minister of defence, sit Mansour and Lieutenant-Colonel Trid. They watch me closely.

'I am not hungry.'

'You're dehydrated, Brotherly Guide, and undernourished. You won't last long like that.'

'I made the sandwich myself,' Trid says, as if to prove that the food is not poisoned. 'I brought a bit of food back with me.'

I push the tray away.

'I am not hungry.'

'Rais——'

'I am not hungry, dammit! What are you going to do, hold my nose and force-feed me?'

'The doctor—'

'I do not give a damn about the doctor. He is not going to teach me how to run my life … What is the time?'

'Nearly 4.30, sir.'

'Should we not have left by now?'

'Colonel Mutassim has not come back yet, sir.'

'We cannot let that stand in our way. It will soon be daylight. How are we going to get out of the city?'

'At present we only have thirty vehicles, sir,' the general argues. 'It won't be enough to break the siege.'

I clap my hands in exasperation.

'The things I have to listen to! I am surrounded by cripples. You are my chief of staff, General, my minister of defence. It is up to you to find the solution. That is your job. Do you want me to do it for you? What have you been doing for the last twenty-four hours? Are you waiting for Gabriel to come and fan you with his wings? Is that it?'

'Gabriel died at Hira, and I've got a canteen to cool me down.'

It is the first time General Abu-Bakr has uttered a profanity in my presence: his piety is beyond belief. It is also the first time he has ever answered me in anything like a critical way. His retort is hardly audible, but somehow it calms me. I understand that my men are under too much stress to deal with my sudden changes of mood, and that the situation demands from me a modicum of wisdom and consideration for my closest collaborators.

The general goes on staring at the floor. He regrets having spoken to me in an inappropriate tone. He knows that I am hypersensitive and that if I sometimes forgive a moment's rudeness, I never forget it.

Mansour starts scratching his head, embarrassed.

As for the lieutenant-colonel, he goes on watching me, a smile playing on his lips.

I study each of them, one at a time, let out a sigh, and ask if there is any news of my son Mutassim.

'No, sir,' the general informs me, in a more conciliatory tone. 'The bombardment has been severe. The colonel has had to stay put.'

'Is he all right?'

'We don't know, sir.'

'What are you waiting for? Send someone to his position immediately.'

'I'll go,' Trid volunteers.

'No, not you. I need you here. Find someone else to go.'

'How can we find the colonel, Rais?' the general says. 'We don't know his position. He has evacuated his garrison.'

'"We don't know, we don't know" — that is all you can say. Ask the driver of the reconnaissance patrol to go.'

'He's wounded, sir.'

'He is pretending. I saw no blood on him. Kick him in the arse, and if he is incapable of holding a steering wheel then put him on the dead man's seat. All he has to do is show whichever officer you send the way to where my son is.'

The general promises to remedy the situation immediately and hastens to carry out my orders. He returns a few minutes later.

'I'm extremely sorry, Rais. The driver has died from his wounds.'

'Good riddance. He was quite obviously a slacker without a brain in his head. The officer can go on his own. He will manage. I wish my son to be back at headquarters before daybreak.'

'I don't think that's a good idea,' Mansour says.

'I suppose you have a better one.'

'The bombardment's over. The rebels are going to redeploy along the line they occupied before their withdrawal. Their scouts will already be back at their forward positions. Our messenger could fall into an ambush. If he's taken alive, they'll torture him until he tells them our position.'

'I asked you if you had another idea.'

The general pulls out his mobile and starts to make a call.

'What the hell are you doing?' I shout.

'I'm trying to get hold of my sons. They're with the colonel.'

'Switch it off, you fool. Our phone signals go via satellite. Do you want to tell the whole world where we are? That was how they managed to track me down at Bab al-Azizia.'

The general apologises profusely and puts his mobile away. I order him to dispatch an officer to my son and dismiss him.

Mansour is hunched in the corner. I do not understand why he stays there, adding fuel to the rage smouldering inside me rather than getting off his arse and helping the general.

'You would be better off commanding your men,' I say to him. 'Leaving them to their own devices will only sap their morale. Get a grip, dammit. You are depressing me.'

He nods his head, hoists his carcass to its feet and shuffles out.

'The laziest of men,' I tell the lieutenant-colonel, once we are alone. 'If you want a man to swagger at your parades you will not find his equal anywhere, but when the going gets tough he will drop you like a hot brick. War reveals so many negative sides to people. A truly sad business!'

'You're hard on him, sir. Mansour has discovered that his nephew was captured by the rebels at Misrata.'

'Mansour's nephew has been captured?'

'Two days ago.'

'Has it been confirmed?'

'That's the rumour that's going around, which of course adds to his uncle's despair. The nephew's a brave lad. I know him. Mansour loves him more than his own children. He feels guilty because he was the one who sent him to Yafran to join Saif al-Islam. According to a survivor, the nephew was caught in an ambush and taken alive.'

'Why was I not told?'

'Bad news only complicates situations, sir. General Abu-Bakr is anxious about his sons too. Mutassim told me they have been missing since he evacuated the garrison.'

'Does the minister know?'

'No.'

I put the Koran down on the couch's arm and rest my chin on my thumb and index finger to think.

'This war has taken everything from us,' I say with a sigh. 'Our children, our grandchildren ... but of all the families in mourning, mine is the one it has exacted the greatest price from. I no longer want to live among my ghosts. A while ago on the roof I talked about paradise and houris and crowns on my tomb. My head was clear, I was lucid and weighing my words. I truly wanted to finish with it all. I was praying for a sniper's bullet.'

'You were just angry.'

I look at the lieutenant-colonel. He holds my gaze, not facing me down, with just that sort of perplexed questioning look schoolboys have when they are not sure they have given their teacher the correct answer.

'Are you afraid of dying, Colonel?'

'Since I made the choice to take up arms I've been guided by one principle: you can't be afraid of dying, because if you are you risk dying of fear. And isn't death the final objective of existence, anyway? Whether you own half the world or live from hand to mouth, it makes no difference; one day you'll be called on to leave everything where it is, all your treasures and your vale of tears, and vanish.'

The vibes this young man gives off are good. They revive me.

'Are you a believer?'

He glances pointedly at the Koran.

'You have nothing to fear,' I reassure him. 'I have an open mind.'

He says, 'In that case, sir, with all the great respect I feel for the devout man I know you to be, I cannot accept the idea that there is a Last Judgement after what we have lived through here on earth. Death can have no value unless it puts a final end to what has ceased to exist.'

'Do you not want to go to paradise?'

'What for? I can't really imagine enjoying, or putting up with, doing the same thing for the whole of eternity. Anything that doesn't come to an end is exhausting or boring or both.'

'If you have no faith, you cannot have any ideals, Colonel.'

'I had faith once, sir. I have no ideals any more. I gave up the first so that I wouldn't have to share it with hypocrites, and the second because I couldn't find anyone to share them with.'

Suddenly emboldened, he adds, 'Do you know why I became a soldier, Brotherly Guide? Because of a speech, or perhaps more of a diatribe. One of yours, sir. I forget what the occasion was or where you delivered it, but there was a phrase that marked me for life. You were furious, wherever it was. With our brothers from the Mashriq and the Maghreb, all the Muslim countries. And you came out with a phrase that should have woken the dead but had no effect on any of those it was aimed at. You said, "There are 350 million sheep out there!"'

This young man has entirely won me over. He knows my anger by heart and has made it his own.

'We don't even produce the spoons we stir our tea with. An army of high rollers who only care about blowing wads of cash or helping ourselves to it, that's what we are. Our great handicap, sir, is the absence of the faculty of thought. It is a tool that's completely foreign to us. And without thought, how can we think about tomorrow, how can we look to the future? We live from day to day, without caring about the generations to come, and one day we're going to wake up without a dinar to our name and ask ourselves, "Where did it all go?"'

He goes on, blushing now, but determined to lance the abscess that has apparently been festering in his mind for years.

'Whatever I've accomplished in the course of my career as a soldier, Rais, I did for you. At no time have I ever had the feeling of working for a national or ideological ideal – or for any sense of identity – because I have never given any credit either to Arab policy-makers who, with every step they take backwards, claim to be advancing against the tide.'

'I'm one of those Arab policy-makers.'

'You have nothing in common with the ones I'm referring to. You're a guide, a real, unique guide, who cannot be replaced. That's why you are alone today.'

'I don't feel my efforts are in vain, Colonel.'

'One can always preach in the desert, sir, but one cannot sow in the sand.'

Two bursts of gunfire ring out from inside the school complex.

The lieutenant-colonel asks me not to leave my room and dashes into the corridor. There is another gunshot and then silence …

I walk over to the window and pull back a piece of tarpaulin, but it does not look out onto the playground. I step into the corridor, listening. Muffled shouts reach me. There is no sound coming from the ground floor, nothing moving. I hear running feet crunching on the gravel of the playground and I wonder if we are being attacked or if there is a mutiny taking place.

'What's going on?' I shout out, in the hope that someone will show themselves on the ground floor.

No one answers me.

Holding firmly on to the banister, I go downstairs one step at a time, keeping a lookout.

Outside the shouts have stopped.

I do not dare venture any further and stay standing halfway down the stairs, ready to go back up to my room and collect my gun at the first sign of danger.

'Who was shooting? Who was shooting?'

The general's voice.

Soldiers burst into the sitting room downstairs. They are carrying two wounded men. Lieutenant-Colonel Trid shows them where to put them.

'Lay them over there. On the floor, there.'

Mansour and the general appear, looking bewildered. They stand over the two bloodied bodies. I join them. Both wounded men are in a critical state. One has been hit in the neck, the other in the chest: he stares at the ceiling, shocked, a gurgling noise coming from his mouth.

'An auxiliary flipped out,' the lieutenant-colonel explains. 'He shot his comrades then turned his weapon on himself. He's lying outside in the yard.'

'What do you mean, flipped out? He might have been trying to kill me.'

'He wanted to go and fight,' another officer says. 'I think it was the shelling that got to him. He'd been in a bad way for several hours. He'd refused to take cover. Then he cracked. He got hold of a weapon and said he couldn't bear to wait any longer and he wanted to fight to the finish. These two tried to disarm him. He shot them, then killed himself.'

He takes me into the courtyard, showing the way with a torch.

A man is lying awkwardly on the ground, a few steps inside the school gate, arms and legs outspread. Half his skull has been blown away. I know who he is from the bracelet around his wrist: it is Mustafa, the orderly who brought me dinner.

13

I order the general and the commander of the People's Guard to ready the troops to withdraw from District Two at the earliest possible opportunity and I invite the lieutenant-colonel to accompany me to my room.

I find it unbearable to be alone, sealed up inside four bare walls that radiate bad luck, telling my beads the way a tortured man counts the final moments of his ordeal.

I pick up my Koran again and attempt to read, but I cannot concentrate. My fasting is starting to fog my vision and to stiffen my muscles. My fingers have become so numb I find it hard to hold the holy book. Waves of dizziness wash over me and I feel like closing my eyes and never opening them again.

The lieutenant-colonel takes a seat on the chair opposite me. His features are creased with fatigue, but his eyes are bright.

I think about Mustafa, the orderly. What did he think he was proving by blowing his brains out? That he was worthy of my respect? Did he have any idea of what he was trying to do? It is strange how men aspire in death to what they have not achieved in life. I try to understand the workings of their minds, and wherever I put my finger on it my understanding is absorbed by the jelly-like surface of their mentalities. Long after thinking I have touched on a definite truth, I realise that I was reading Braille back to front and that the mysteries I was convinced I had unravelled have instead swallowed me whole.

Just now, on the roof, I too wanted death to give me what life is threatening to take away from me: my honour, my legitimacy as sovereign, my courage as a free man. I was ready to die a hero to keep my legend safe. There was no play-acting. By exposing myself on the parapet I wanted to be my own trophy, to claim all of my prestige. There is no shame in being beaten. Defeat has a merit of its own: it is proof that you fought. Only those who desert deserve no consideration, even less so if there are attenuating circumstances ... What did my subordinates think when they saw me 'making a spectacle of myself'? Did they think I had gone mad? I admit that I was being ridiculous – I can only see the inappropriateness of my fury now that a man who feared losing my trust has chosen to lose everything else with it – but I do not regret having bawled out my resolve loud and long.

Life is so complicated. And crazy. It is only a matter of months since the West, having cast aside all sense of shame, was rolling out the red carpet, showering me with honours, garlanding my colonel's epaulettes with laurels. They let me pitch my tent next to the Champs-Élysées, excusing my boorishness, closing their eyes to my 'outrages'. And today they are hunting me down on my own territory like an ordinary convict on the run. Strange the way time deals out these sudden reversals. One day you are idolised, the next an object of revulsion; one day the predator, the next the prey. You trust the Voice that deifies you in your heart of hearts and then one fine day, without warning, you find yourself hiding in a corner, naked and defenceless, without a friend in the world. In the immense solitude of my status as sovereign, where no one could keep me company, I never dismissed the possibility of being assassinated or overthrown. That is the price of absolute sovereignty, particularly the sort that one has usurped by force. The spectre of sin and the dread of treason are hardly a millimetre apart. You live with an alarm bell implanted inside your brain. Asleep or awake, whether you are engaged in private reflection or out making your presence felt, you are always on your guard. A fraction of a second's inattention, and everything that once was is no more. There is no more extreme stress than that of being a sovereign – it is an intensified, obsessional, permanent stress, close to that of those beasts that you see in nature documentaries gasping for water, unable to quench their thirst at a watering hole without looking around them a dozen times, their ears pricked, their sense of smell filtering the air the way one sniffs for signs of a deadly gas. Yet never did I envisage a fall from grace as crude as this. To end up in a disused school, surrounded by mobs of rebel troops, in a town as third-rate as they come? How can I come to terms with falling so low, me, the leader whose very moon felt cramped in the infinite heavens! Even if I were to kill thousands of insurgents with my bare hands, it would not alleviate the sorrow that gnaws at my heart like a cancer. I feel absolutely swindled and betrayed; even the Voice that once sang inside me has fallen silent. The silence that now fills my being frightens me as much as a ghost in the night.

My watch says five o'clock.

Engines are revving up in the school precinct.

With a finger I pull back the tarpaulin covering the window to look outside.

'You can pull it down, sir,' Lieutenant-Colonel Trid says. 'We haven't got anything to hide any more.'

'Really?'

'Let me do it. You might get dirty.'

He asks me to step away before tugging at the tarpaulin, which falls in a cloud of dust.

Outside, day has no need to break. District Two, with its smoking ruins and burning buildings, is a step ahead of it.

Sirte's pyres might be mistaken for spears of sunlight, but it will not stop night from following day.

Here and there sub-machine guns start chattering at each other again. Men are reawakening to their drama. Night has brought them no wiser counsel.

In the sky, a harbinger still of deadly storms, drones are drifting in lazy circles, vultures in search of the dying.

Everything gives the impression that the town is merely picking itself out of its rubble in order to fall back into it any minute now. Dawn, bled white this morning, only exposes a filthy, festering wound.

'We are not going to make it out this time, Colonel.'

'Why do you say that, sir?'

'My instinct has gone dead. There is a strange silence inside me, and it is a bad sign. I shall not surrender, but I shall not see another day break.'

'I've often been trapped, sir. Thought it was all over. In Mali, once, near Aguelhok, the army had surrounded us. I was with the leader of the Azawad rebels and three of his lieutenants in a hut, without food or water, with a handful of ammunition and our prayers, convinced that these were our last hours on earth. Then a sandstorm blew up. We got out of the hut and slipped straight through the enemy lines.'

'There will be no sandstorm today.'

I walk back to the couch and slump onto it.

'We are going to lose the war, Colonel.'

'It's Libya that will have lost you, Brotherly Guide.'

'It amounts to the same thing.'

'In one sense.'

'And the other?'

He does not answer.

'There is only one sense, Colonel. The one that describes our destiny. We are merely actors; we play roles that we have not necessarily chosen and we are not allowed to consult the script.'

'You have made history, Rais.'

'False. It is history that has made me. When I glance over my shoulder, to take stock of my life, I realise that nothing is the result of my will, or of my military accomplishments, or the strokes of luck that have got me out of trouble. I tell myself, why complicate life if everything is preordained? There is someone up there who knows what He is doing ... But in the last few days I have begun to wonder whether He has already turned the page. Perhaps He has chosen another pawn to play with.'

I pick up the Koran and replace it immediately.

'You see, Colonel? Even the most wonderful fairy tales, when they are reinvented as soap opera, end up being boring. That must be what has happened to the One up there. He has lost His train of thought where I am concerned. He does not even feel like knowing the end of the story any more.'

The lieutenant-colonel holds out the bar of chocolate.

'There's magnesium in it, sir. You need to keep your strength up.'

'I am not hungry.'

'Please …'

'I am a mystic. Fasting suits me perfectly. It helps keep my mind clear when things refuse to go right.'

He does not press the point and goes back to sit on his chair.

This lad is outstanding. He has class, depth, an Olympian calm that keeps increasing his stature in my eyes, and – the rarest of virtues – he is entirely natural. He is aware of the great esteem in which I hold him, but that special favour has not spoilt him. Others would have taken endless advantage of it; he tucks it away in his heart like something precious, a holy gift that he could not expose to the air without damaging it.

'What would you like to have accomplished that you have not had the opportunity to achieve yet, Colonel?'

He reflects for a moment or two, then, in a barely audible voice, he says, 'To be loved madly.'

'Are you not loved enough?'

'My wife complains that she has married a ghost because of my continual absences, and my comrades are all wildly jealous of me. Every time I go on a mission they pray I won't come back.'

'That is normal with your comrades. They are cross

with you for overtaking them and detest you because they know they will never be half the man you are. But that cannot be the case with your wife. If she is jealous, unlike your colleagues she is also praying day and night for you to come home to her.'

'She knows I'm faithful to her.'

'No one knows that kind of thing. However much we trust the one we love, when they are not there doubt stalks us everywhere, like our shadow.'

'I haven't been unfaithful to her once in eight years of marriage.'

'It will come. You are handsome, as brilliant as it is possible to be, and ahead of all your intake. Any woman would fall for you. Women are more dazzled by rank than muscles.'

'Not all, Brotherly Guide.'

'How do you know? There are bedroom secrets that faithful husbands can never dream of.'

He raises his hands in surrender.

'I hope there's nothing for me to dream of.'

'That does not depend on you.'

He has run out of arguments and laughs.

His good mood calms me a little.

'Apart from being loved, what else would be your dearest accomplishment?'

He places his hands over his nose and reflects. His eyes are bright as he says, 'My grandfather was a shepherd. He had no education, but he had a very good philosophy of life. I've never known anyone so comfortable with their poverty. The smallest thing could make him happy. When luck was on his side, for my grandfather everything was good. You had to see things as they were, not as you wanted them to be. In his eyes, just being alive was an extraordinary stroke of luck and no hardship could take that away. I remember he did nothing apart from look after his sheep, just vegetated and wore the same rags summer and winter. When I went to find him to suggest that he came and lived with my little family at Ajdabiya, in a nice villa that overlooked the sea, he just shook his head. Nothing in the world could have made him want to leave his tent that he'd pitched in the middle of nowhere.'

'He was wrong.'

'Maybe, but he was like that, my grandfather. He had decided to feel good the way he was, never going to much trouble. He was happy and rich in the joys he shared with the people he loved. Every morning he was up at first light to watch the sky catch fire. He said he didn't need anything else ... That's the feat I'd like to have accomplished, sir. To be like my grandfather: a man never annoyed by anything, who possessed just the modest happiness that came from feeling comfortable with a life of complete frugality.'

'I shall never understand how some people can

pretend that resignation is the same as humility.'

I find the lieutenant-colonel touching in his naivety and wonder what will become of him. I would like him to survive this. He is so young, so handsome and authentic. He embodies the Libyan army I dreamt of, the officer who would outlive me, to carry on my teachings and deliver eulogies to my glory at every commemoration.

'Do you know van Gogh, Colonel?'

'Of course. He sliced off his ear so that the red on his canvas would be as vivid as his pain.'

'Someone once told me that he mutilated himself because of a romance that went wrong.'

He opens his arms.

'Every genius has his own fantasies, sir. You said yourself that there is no truth except death, and that it is lies that shape life.'

'I do not remember having said such a thing.'

'Many other quotations will be attributed to you in the future, Brotherly Guide. Just as we attribute anonymous poems to Al-Mutanabbi. It is part and parcel of mythology.'

'Do you believe that people will remember me?'

'For as long as this country is called Libya.'

'And what will they remember about me?'

'You will have followers, and a mass of detractors. The former will revere you, the latter reproach you for everything you have accomplished, because they have done so little with their lives. One thing is certain, that you will be missed by the majority of our people.'

'I do not think so, Colonel. That people you speak of has no more memory than any hothead – how otherwise do you explain that it seeks my downfall after what I have done for it?'

The colonel runs his hand through his hair. A lock of hair flops onto his brow, emphasising a little more his young centurion's charm. He contemplates his spotless white hands before speaking.

'When I was doing a course at Vystrel Academy, near Moscow, I made friends with some of the Russians there. They were young officers or young cadres, straight out of university. They went around with the latest mobile phones, drove the most fashionable 4×4s, wore perfume from Dior and designer clothes and had dinner in chic restaurants that they'd booked online with their sophisticated laptops. They were today's people, rich and in a hurry. They hadn't known the period of scarcity, the *chorni khleb*, the endless queues outside shops whose shelves were practically empty, the institutionalised spying at post offices and prison sentences for wearing a pair of jeans you'd bought on the black market. Yet when they drank so much vodka that they couldn't tell a fork from a rake, they went on and on about how bad everything was, how the country was going to the dogs, how the state structures were pathetic and the oligarchs' corruption intolerable, and how much they missed Stalin's iron hand ... It's the same everywhere, Brotherly Guide. In Chile they miss Pinochet, in Spain they miss Franco, in Iraq Saddam, in China Mao, the same way they miss Mubarak in Egypt and Genghis Khan in Mongolia.'

'What image will they have of me? Will I be their guide or their tyrant?'

'You're not a tyrant. You did exactly what needed to be done. There are two sorts of people. People who work with their heads and people who need a big stick. Our people needed a big stick.'

I cannot agree with him.

I acknowledge that I treated those who became dissidents without mercy. How else could I have responded? To rule over people requires a culture that is compatible with a single medium: blood. Without blood, a throne is a potential gallows. To protect mine, I took a leaf out of the chameleon's book: I walked with one eye looking ahead, the other behind, my step calibrated to the millimetre, my speech moralistic and as unhesitating as lightning. The moment I melted into the background, I became part of the background ...

'The only people I clamped down on were traitors, Colonel. I loved and protected my people.'

'You shouldn't have, Rais. You cosseted them too much and it made them lazy and cunning. They wallowed in their sense of entitlement to the point where they couldn't be bothered to shoo a fly off a cake any more. They thought work, knowledge, ambition were a waste of time. Why worry about anything when the Brotherly Guide is there to think for everyone? The average Libyan has no idea of how generous you've been to him. He's just taken advantage of you. He thought he was a little prince and expected it to last for ever. From the moment he sees that people are working so he doesn't have to, operating his machines so he can knock off, why should he wait for a lunch break? He gets tired just looking at his Africans working like dogs for him. Now he's trying to prove he's worth more than he was originally valued at, and so how does he do it? By biting the hand that fed him. If you'll allow me, sir, I think you should have treated your people the same way you treated your dissidents. They are not worth the time and concern you have lavished on them, sir. They're a nation of shopkeepers and smugglers who only know how to do dodgy deals and doss around. Tomorrow's Libyans will miss you the way that they miss Stalin in Russia, because with the gang we've got here, knocking our cities flat and lynching its heroes in public, our grandchildren are going to inherit a country that's been handed over to puppets and incompetents.'

I feel both hurt and relieved by the lieutenant-colonel's words.

'What I like about you, my boy, even more than your

courage, is your frankness. Not one of my ministers or concubines has ever opened my eyes to the reality you have just described. Every one of them flattered me that I had made, out of a rabble of Bedouins, the proudest people on earth.'

'They weren't lying to you. From a ragtag of tribes who were all hostile to each other you made a single body and a single spirit. But the real truth was more than that.'

'Why was it hidden from me?'

'Because it wasn't nice, sir.'

At that moment the bedroom door opens with a crash. It is Mansour who has come to brief us, breathless and feverish, his face flushed. He informs us that the officer ordered to contact Mutassim has returned and that it is time for us to set out.

I turn to the colonel.

'It is the moment of truth.'

14

On the ground floor there is general mobilisation. Soldiers are running in all directions. Officers are shouting to gee themselves up and manhandling the slower men, caught off guard by the turn of events.

I detest messes. One breeds another; they make my nervous tension worse.

I suspect the general of not having briefed his subordinates. I look for him in the mêlée but cannot see him anywhere.

Mansour brings over to me the officer whose return has sparked everything off. He is young, probably only just out of the Academy. He salutes me and practically falls over, unnerved by the expression I must have on my face.

'Where is my son?'

'He is on his way, sir.'

'You have seen him?'

'Yes, sir.'

'Personally?'

'Absolutely, sir. He handed over to me the twenty vehicles I've brought back with me and ordered me to tell you that we must leave at once.'

'Why did he not come with you?'

'He is commanding the third – the last – section of the convoy. At least thirty vehicles. It's being slowed down by the two Shilka batteries.'

'Is he safe and sound?'

'Yes, sir. He says he'll catch us up en route, after we're clear of District Two.'

My armoured 4×4 is lined up in the courtyard. Lieutenant-Colonel Trid is organising the column, summoning the drivers and issuing orders about the procedure to follow.

'There will be four cars in front for reconnaissance. I'll be in the fifth vehicle, which will travel two hundred metres back. The rais will be in the sixth. On no account are you to stop if you are attacked. If I leave the convoy, you will follow me. Do not let me out of your sight for a second. You are there to ensure the rais's safety at all times.'

The drivers click their heels and return to their vehicles.

Mansour and I take our seats in the armoured 4×4.

'Where is the general?'

'He went to see if his two sons had arrived,' the Guard commander informs me.

'Get him. I want him to travel with us.'

Someone runs to find the general. The minutes drag on. I swear in the back of the 4×4, thump the back of the driver's seat.

Abu-Bakr finally arrives, panting and sweating.

'Where did you get to, damn you?'

'I was looking for my sons.'

'Now is not the time. Get in the front; everyone is waiting for you.'

As soon as the general climbs into the 4×4, the convoy sets off.

We drive out of the school in an almighty roar. In their haste vehicles drive into each other, some scrambling onto the pavement to get to their place in the column as fast as they can.

The convoy sorts itself into a disciplined file as it turns onto the ring road that leads to the coast. As we reach the first junction, I realise I have left my Koran and my prayer beads in my room.

We drive, exposed, along the coast road, at the mercy of ambushes and air raids.

Rarely has the day been so radiant. Despite the pall of smoke from the fires, it has a dazzling clarity. It feels as though the sun has chosen the traitors' side – it illuminates me like a target.

I am not calm, but I am not excessively concerned. I have no idea where they are taking me or what is waiting for me around the next bend, yet I do not have the feeling that it is essential to know either of these things. What would it change?

Mansour, on my right, is tense. He hugs his gun as

though clinging to a rope that will pull him out of the chasm his silence has become. His fingers are white at the joints. Immense olive-coloured bags darken the skin under his eyes. I suspect he is praying as profoundly as he has ever prayed.

Inside the cabin the burbling of the engine is a gloomy sound.

The general looks in the rear-view mirror to see if there is any sign of the third section of the convoy, the one commanded by my son, in which he hopes he will see his two sons again.

'Can you see anything?'

'Not yet, Rais.'

'Why did Mutassim want to overload himself with the Shilkas?' Mansour grumbles. 'They're tracked and too heavy: they're going to slow us down. In any case, what can 37s do against the coalition's planes? Their range is nowhere near great enough. You could use them for hunting bustards, and that's all.'

'They're better than nothing,' the general says.

'They're not even credible as decoration,' Mansour persists. 'Those vultures carrying out the air strikes are using long-range weapons. They don't have to come anywhere near our coastline.'

I prefer not to listen to them.

I try to think of nothing; I dive deep inside myself in search of that Voice that promised me mountains and marvels when I was a disillusioned lieutenant and beginning to stink in the shadow of my own bitterness, the Voice that soothed and graced my solitude with its promises and challenges. Where has it gone? Why has it fallen silent? I visualise it curled up somewhere in the blackness that is slowly overtaking me, but I find only the echo of my prayers. The Voice has left the ship, and there is no one at the helm.

I am alone with destiny, and destiny is looking elsewhere.

Even Sirte, the city of my adolescence – the cradle of my revolution – has turned its back on me.

There was a time when its squares and stadiums teemed with people come to acclaim me. Pavements and platforms overflowed with fervour and pennants. People held up portraits of me and sang my praises until they were hoarse. It was here, in this city where memories are already being rewritten, that I took an oath to bring fate to her knees. Then it was just a quiet little medina that did not know how to sell itself or make itself desirable. Along its corniche the wealthy dreamt of the casinos that glittered on the Mediterranean's northern shore; at its roadsides the poor dreamt of nothing, having been stripped of everything. A gulf as deep as an abyss kept the two classes so far apart that when they happened to pass each other in the street they did not even see one another; they went on their respective ways like ghosts, each in their parallel world. I remember the low-class cafés that stank of piss and privation, the souks infested with beggars and scrawny pickpockets, the kids with heads swollen with ulcers who rolled in the dust giggling as if they were possessed, their noses streaming and their pus-clogged eyes swarming with flies; I can still smell the sickening stenches that rose from the open sewers, see the women in rags chanting in doorways in voices more tragic than any funeral dirge, the stray dogs roaming the rubbish tips with their fangs bared, trying to assuage their hunger, the old people pinned to the walls like scarecrows nobody wanted, the alleys that were as narrow and dark as twisted minds. It was here, in this town, that I grabbed a police officer by the throat when I saw him slap a man in front of his children just because he asked for directions. I have never forgotten the expression on those children's faces; nothing has ever infuriated me more. It was boom time for feudalists, for middle-class Muslims who spoke Italian, from their grand cars that did not stop when they ran pedestrians over.

And I said, 'Enough!'

And I raised my voice and said, 'Death to the king!'

And I founded a republic and brought justice back.

It was right here, in this city that is turning its back on its values, that I knocked down those stinking cafés, demolished the slums, put up buildings taller than towers, built hospitals equipped with ultra-modern facilities, attractive sparkling shops like aquariums, handsome esplanades and mosaic fountains; I laid out boulevards as wide as parade grounds and turned empty lots into municipal gardens where dreams and everyday joys merged.

Thanks to who?

Thanks to me, and me alone, father of the revolution, the Ghous clan's chosen one, come from the desert to sow tranquillity in the hearts and minds of the people.

I was Moses, come down from the mountain with a green book as my tablet.

Everything I did worked.

The champions of Arab nationalism glorified me at the tops of their voices, the leaders of the Third World ate out of my hand, African presidents quenched their thirst from my lips, apprentice revolutionaries kissed my brow and were transported into ecstasy; all the children of the free world took pride in being associated with me.

Was there anyone who did not praise Muammar to the skies, scourge of kings and hunter of eagles, the Bedouin of Fezzan crowned rais at the age of twenty-seven?

I was young, handsome, proud, and such a pheno-menon that I only had to pick up any old pebble for it to become the philosopher's stone.

And what do I see today? I, the miracle-maker whose charisma bewitched women? What do I see after all my Pharaonic creations, all my crowning achievements? A town handed over to the pillage and vandalism of an army of jinn, villas with their shutters blown off, devastated squares, desecrated buildings and burnt-out cars – a city despoiled as far as the eye can see.

They have crossed out my slogans, disfigured the portraits of me that decorated the façades of buildings: I can see one on a billboard, slashed with a bayonet and smeared with excrement.

Is that how people show love for their guide? Did this people love me sincerely, or was it merely a mirror reflecting back to me my own exaggerated narcissism?

No, they could not identify with me; it was I who saw myself in them, taking their clamour at face value. Now I know: the people of Libya do not know very much about love. They lied to me, just as the profiteers and my mistresses mocked me. I was their open sesame: they sweet-talked me into holding the candle for them while they stuffed their pockets at my expense. From a pathetic rabble I made a happy and prosperous nation, and look at the thanks I get. I feared treachery inside my palaces, but it was creeping up on me unsuspected in the towns and villages. Lieutenant-Colonel Trid was not wrong: my people are a gang. Unlike me, who lived entrenched in my bunkers, Trid is a field soldier.

He evolved among the people, got to know them inside out. I should have dealt with them the way I dealt with dissidents, been more severe with them, distrusted them more. Dissidents betray themselves; the people betrayed me instead. If I had my time again, I would exterminate half the nation. Lock them up in camps to show them what real work is, and watch them die in the attempt; hang the rest at the roadside to encourage the others. Stalin haunted the dreams of good and bad alike, great and small, did he not? He died in his bed, showered with laurels, and was so mourned by his people they drowned in their own tears. Stockholm syndrome is the only remedy for nations full of cheats.

How dare they knife me in the back?

Libya owes me everything. The reason it is going up in smoke today is because it is unworthy of my goodness. Go on, go up in smoke, accursed country. Your belly is barren, there will be no phoenix rising from your ashes.

If a forest is to regrow, it first has to burn, that is what fools say.

Drivel!

There are forests that never recover from their destruction. They go up in flames like those monks who set themselves alight, and no shoot ever grows from their ashes.

One day mythology will say of Libya that it was a forest born from the hairs on the head of a providential figure, himself the product of a divine dream, beneath a carnival sky, bearing a green standard that flutters in the wind and a book the same colour that contains, like holy verses, both the prayers I offered and those I granted so that my homeland, which became my child, should not suffer either the thunderbolts of demons or the flames of incendiaries.

Libya is my magic trick, my own Olympus. Here in my realm, where I have been the humblest of sovereigns, the trees have grown straight since they stood to attention at the sound of my trumpets. Here, in the land of poets and of scimitars, every flower that blooms blooms because it trusts me, every stream that bubbles up between the pebbles tries to flow to me, every baby bird that cheeps in its nest praises me.

What happened, so suddenly, to turn the ayah on its head, to make my subjects drown out my words with their own?

The sorrow of it!

I am like God. The world I made has turned against me.

15

Abu-Bakr is restless in the front seat, twisting his head, staring in the rear-view mirror and then turning to look over his shoulder. For the last ten minutes we have been driving through empty suburbs. Looted shops, houses without doors and windows, railings and shutters banging in the silence and the burnt-out shells of cars bear witness to the vandals' ferocity. They have even torn down the few trees that line the roadside.

It feels as though we are in a town that has died.

On the façade of one building a black flag flutters as a sign of mourning.

Farewell, Sirte. Nothing will ever be as it was for you. Your celebrations will feel like funerals and your banquets taste of ashes. But when you are asked what you did with your talents do not, I beg you, lower your head and point an accusatory finger at the barbarians who ravish you today. Above all, say nothing, because it is you yourself who have despoiled your talents.

We are driving at speed, yet I have the feeling we are running on the spot, so much does each part of town look the same as the last. On pavements strewn with debris and rubble, large dark stains show the places where tyres have been burnt, where people built barricades and were attacked and where men were lynched before being doused in petrol and set on fire. A horrible smell of cremation hangs in the air, which is laden with omens of apocalypse.

Since leaving the school we have not seen one living being, apart from dogs fleeing the fighting, and stray cats. The only human trace we have glimpsed is the body of a soldier hanged from a lamppost, his trousers around his ankles, his penis amputated.

'What's that cloud of dust way back there?' the general asks the driver.

The driver adjusts his wing mirror.

'It looks like the Shilkas, General. It must be Colonel Mutassim's unit.'

The general sits back, relieved. As he turns to me to see if I am happy that my son is joining us at last, gunfire rings out. A rebel roadblock ahead. The leading cars in the column turn sharply southwards; the rest of the convoy follows in a thunder of machine-gun fire. A pickup sways under the impact of the bullets, swerves and crashes into a ditch. Its occupants leap out and return fire to cover each other; they are immediately shot.

Our driver floors the 4×4, heading south.

The general hands me a helmet and body armour.

'The shit's hitting the fan,' Mansour groans.

An explosion suddenly slows us. Ahead vehicles are peeling off right and left. The second 4×4 of my personal bodyguard is in flames.

Lieutenant-Colonel Trid sounds his horn, his arm out of the window signalling the drivers to keep moving.

We drive past the burning 4×4. One of the rear doors is lying on the road next to a dismembered torso. Inside the cabin the occupants are on fire where they sit, killed instantly.

'The road's mined,' the general shouts.

'A mine would have destroyed the road,' Mansour says, 'but the 4×4 was stopped dead. That means an air strike. A drone probably.'

Lieutenant-Colonel Trid's car draws level with the leading vehicle; I see him order the driver to accelerate before he lets two cars pass him and rejoins the convoy in front of my armoured 4×4.

Behind us part of the convoy has halted because of the crash or possibly mechanical problems; the other half is overtaking in any way it can in an effort to catch up with us.

Mansour puts his hand on my knee to comfort me.

'Remove your hand,' I order him. 'Whatever you do, do not touch me. I have not forgotten the way you behaved yesterday.'

He does not take his hand away but presses my knee more firmly.

'Muammar, my brother, master, guide, we're going to die. What is the point of leaving each other still angry about things that don't matter?'

'We're going to get out of this mess,' the general shouts at him. 'God is with us.'

'God has changed sides, my poor Abu-Bakr,' Mansour sighs. 'He's with our enemies now, leaving us only our eyes to weep with.'

I elbow him hard in the ribs to make him shut up.

'Silence, bird of ill omen.'

Behind us there is disarray. Some vehicles are turning back, others are scattering down minor roads. Sporadic explosions can be heard, then longer salvoes.

'Are we being attacked, General?'

'I don't think so, Rais.'

'Our men are panicking,' Mansour explains. 'They're firing at random because they don't know what's going on. They'll kill each other without realising it.'

The lieutenant-colonel has also seen the chaos overtaking the second part of the convoy. He turns his car round to try to restore some order to the column, realises the situation is deteriorating, and returns to us. With a hand he invites our driver to follow him.

We negotiate a roundabout to go back the way we have come, doubling back as far as the 4×4 hit by the air strike, then turn down an avenue cratered with holes. The general signals to me that a third of the convoy has got lost. I turn round to check and can see only twenty or so vehicles weaving along behind us.

'We have to restore some order here, General, otherwise we shall get bogged down.'

'There is a barracks not far from here,' he says.

'Head for it.'

We overtake the lieutenant-colonel's car to direct him to the barracks. But the complex is occupied by militiamen. They meet our arrival with 12.7 mm machine guns and anti-tank rockets. We retreat in indescribable chaos. A deafening roar comes from overhead. I just have time to see two fighters streak across the sky like meteorites, then two bombs hit the column right in the middle. Behind us vehicles start exploding in a chain reaction, like Chinese firecrackers. A human arm, on fire, bounces off the windscreen of my 4×4. The convoy is in utter confusion. Men abandon their vehicles and flee in all directions.

There are oil drums blocking the avenue. We turn onto a road that runs parallel.

'They're drawing us into a trap,' Mansour warns us. 'Let's turn back.'

'Where to?' Abu-Bakr curses.

'To the Hotel Mahari.'

'It's too risky.'

'It's less risky than driving like maniacs into the unknown.'

Lieutenant-Colonel Trid's car brakes. Too late to avoid the spikes scattered across the road, his driver loses control; my 4×4 rams him. The driver and the general are stunned by the airbags. Mansour opens the door, jumps down, shooting as he goes two militiamen attracted by the collision. I grab my Kalashnikov and get out of the vehicle after him. The still groggy driver helps the general out. We start running in no particular direction. My soldiers fire blindly. The area is stiff with rebels. We are locked down. Skirmishing starts in the side streets. Shouts of 'Allāhu Akbar' are punctuated by interminable volleys. The convoy's third section, commanded by my son, tries to break through to join us, but is stopped by mortar fire. Jets of fire and steel are tearing my troops to shreds. Mansour has disappeared. Lieutenant-Colonel Trid's face is covered in blood. He gestures to me to put my head down and follow a low wall to where he is. My personal bodyguard regroups around me. Nearby, on the other side of the wall, a pickup mounted with a heavy machine gun is spraying fire. Its exhaust clouds choke the air. My throat is burning. Trid aims at the gunner and blows his head off. We attack the pickup from the rear and take it out with the second grenade. I see the driver writhing inside it as the flames consume him.

To our left, a group of about fifty soldiers is holding several groups of rebels at bay. I can see my son

Mutassim directing the operation. He has seen me too, and gestures to me to stay where I am. The rebels are trying to outflank us to prevent us getting into a residential area. The exchanges of gunfire are becoming more intense. Mortar shells are targeting our position to dislodge us. One falls thirty metres from where we are sheltering, but fails to explode. Mutassim manages to crawl over to me. I am so happy to see him in the flesh that I do not spot the sniper taking aim opposite. A round whistles past my ear, forcing me to the ground.

'We have to pull out,' my son says. 'I've sent a company to create a diversion further down. It won't hold out for more than an hour. The rebels are constantly being reinforced. There'll be tanks here soon and the whole sector will be surrounded. We need to fall back to the north. It's the only gap left.'

The sniper is keeping us flat on our stomachs. We cannot lift our heads. Mutassim takes two guards with him and, hugging the wall, creeps into a garden. A grenade detonates and the gunfire opposite stops. Mutassim comes back with one guard, the other is dead.

We run towards a building that explodes before we reach it and retreat under falling shrapnel. Some soldiers signal to us to join them in a villa. The general has sprained his ankle; a guard helps him run. The villa is fifty metres away, but it feels as if it is at the end of the earth. Mutassim pushes me ahead of him. We succeed in reaching it, losing two men on the way. The rebels have discovered us; they converge on our location, heavily armed pickups in support. Our soldiers try to cover us from the balconies; they are mown down in a single sweep of fire. We go into the villa, which is already crumbling under a hail of missiles. The windows are smashed, the walls are shredded by large-calibre rounds. Shells start to rain down on us, turning our refuge into a hell. The building is choked with dust and smoke. The screams of the wounded can be heard upstairs. A man teeters at the top of the stairs, one arm torn off, his face blackened, then collapses and crashes down the stairs to the ground floor. He rolls almost to my feet, grimaces at me and breathes his last, his eyes bulging. The rebels are very close now; some have scaled the wall of the compound and are crawling through the garden. My guards spray them with fire.

Mutassim tells me that the building will not withstand mortars or anti-aircraft guns and that we must evacuate.

'I'm going to reconnoitre,' he says. 'I've seen some orchards at the back. Hold on till I get back.'

He calls a squad together to go with him and leaves by the service door. It is the last time I will see him. A few minutes later, just two of his men return.

'The colonel has been wounded,' one of them tells me.

'And you left him there?'

'We couldn't do anything, sir. We lost six men trying to bring him back, but the rebels took him alive.'

I no longer feel like waiting for anything. Everything seems unnatural, perverse and pointless to me. Life or death, what's the difference? My son's in the hands of barbarians. I don't dare imagine the fate that awaits him. A fathomless rage grips me. The general realises that I'm about to give up on everything, combat, resistance, escape. He clutches me by the arm and drags me behind him to the service door. I run, unaware of what I'm doing; I don't care what might happen to me. I'm not even conscious of the shots that follow us. I can vaguely see fields ahead of me. My helmet comes unfastened and falls off; I don't pick it up. I only know that I'm running, that my chest is burning, that my heart's about to burst.

Rebels intercept us on some open ground. My guards shelter me behind a pile of earth. The gunfire is continuous. One of my men falls backwards, his hand torn off. The grenade he tried to throw at our opponents clipped the parapet and bounced back to explode in the middle of our group. The general was hit worst: he lies next to me with his stomach open and his guts spilling out. He wants to say something to me but cannot speak. His face turns ashen, his mouth stops moving; I think he has just died.

Everything that begins on earth must come to an end one day. That is the law.

Life is only a dream to which our death sounds the reveille, my uncle used to say to comfort himself. What matters is not what you take with you, but what you leave behind.

I stand up, pull off my body armour, throw it down, leave my gun where it is and start running across the fields, praying for a burst of gunfire to mow me down and catapult me far, far away from this debauched world.

A large agricultural drainage pipe appears in front of me. I cannot say why I decided to hide myself in it.

16

Running feet approach, pass close by my hiding place, fade away. My hands are trembling, my knees threatening to give way; the mad dash has exhausted me. I crouch in the half-darkness, overcome with dizziness and nausea; the thumping of my heart sounds so loud I am afraid it will be heard by my pursuers.

I feel ashamed at having turned into a target, a piece of game, I, Muammar Gaddafi, thorn in the side of the all-powerful; I am ashamed at having fled from a bunch of brats and run like a maniac across the fields; I am ashamed at having been reduced to hiding in a drainage pipe, I who jabbed my finger at the lectern at the UN to warn presidents and kings.

I feel like crying but the tears refuse to come; I feel like stepping into the open and shouting, 'I am here,' but I do not dare move a muscle. My one-time courage has deserted me, my suicidally reckless charisma is a thing of the ancient past.

I believed myself predestined to a sumptuous end. When I happened to think about death, I used to visualise myself lying in my patriarchal bed, surrounded by my family and most loyal subjects. I imagined my body laid out in the presidential palace, hung with wreaths and flags, with leaders and representatives come from the four corners of the planet to observe long minutes of silence before my garlanded remains, and my coffin on a tank draped with banners processing down Tripoli's boulevards followed by millions of inconsolable Libyans. At the cemetery, full to overflowing, I heard the imams declaiming the most impossibly moving suras for my soul's repose and, to the spadefuls of earth bearing me away from my people's affection, the salute in reply of hundreds of cannon announcing to the whole world that the unforgettable Muammar was no more.

I was wrong.

If only I had listened to Hugo Chávez when he offered me his protection: at this moment I would be somewhere in Venezuela, arranging my declining years to perfection and in utter peace and tranquillity, instead of awaiting my executioners at the bottom of a drain. How could I have been so stupid?

Pride is invulnerable to reason. When you have ruled over peoples, you sit on your cloud and forget reality. But what exactly have you ruled over? To what purpose? In the final analysis, power is a misunderstanding: you think you know, then you realise you have made a thumping mistake. Instead of going back and redoing it properly, you dig your heels in and see things the way you would like them to be. You deal with the unthinkable as best you can and cling to your fancies, convinced that if you were to let go all hell would break loose.

And now, paradoxically, all hell has broken loose because I did not let go.

I stare at the light at the end of the tunnel, unable to breathe.

I refuse to think about my son, about what I myself will go through; I empty my head; I must not torment myself.

The minutes pass.

I hear bursts of gunfire that intensify, rockets replying to grenades, vehicles coming and going in a screech of tyres.

I am alone.

Alone in the world.

Left high and dry by my guardian angels and the marabouts who predicted a thousand victories for me in return for a few extra noughts on their cheques.

Where have my servants gone, my Amazons and my supporters who were so ardent they would whip themselves in public to show their devotion to the world? ... Vanished into thin air! *Puff!* Melted into the background. Did they really exist? And my people, once loyal to my cause, standing behind me for better or worse, who took an oath to follow me wherever the Voice led me, what do they hope to raise over my bones?

My people have lied to me from the start, since that morning when on the radio from Benghazi I broke their chains and gave them back their dignity. My people have never loved me, they have just flattered me to receive my gifts, following the example of my courtesans, my kin and my whores.

I should have known: a sovereign can never have friends, he just has enemies who plot behind his back and opportunists he keeps close to his heart the way you nourish a viper in your bosom.

I should have listened to Bassem Tanout, a Libyan poet I knew a very long time ago, in London, during my training with the British Army Staff. He was a maverick, a lovely man as frank and open as a child's laughter. He lived in exile: his country was his dog-eared library of books and a wad of paper that he covered with lines of rebellious verse. He came back to Libya the day after the coup and we continued to meet. In the early years of my rule he regularly came to my house. Then the intervals between his visits started to get longer. I did not see him any more. He declined my official invitations, did not respond to my letters. I decided that some harm must have come to him and I launched a search to find him. One night my agents brought him to me. As poets go, he did not look like much. He was as crumpled as his clothes; you could smell the alcohol on him a mile away and he was shivering like a junkie in withdrawal. When I asked him if he had problems, he retorted that I was his problem. 'You disappoint me, Muammar,' he announced from the heights of his inebriation. 'You're in the process of destroying with your left hand what you have built with your right. Don't rely on the people's clamour. The people are a siren song. Their fervour is a pernicious addiction. It is the vice of choice for exalted egos, their nirvana for a night and then their certain downfall.' I was so wounded by his words that I banished him from my sight. For weeks afterwards his reproaches obsessed me. To ward them off I locked their author up in a dungeon. Three days after his arrest his gaolers found him hanged in his cell, a verse from Omar Khayyam carved on the wall as his legacy.

Thinking back to that time, as yesterday's ovations turn into the baying of the arena, Bassem Tanout is the one and only friend I have ever had.

Other people come back to me. Each more crippled than the next. They drag themselves over the flagstones that pave the prison yards I consigned them to. All have the same look about them, the look that says one-way ticket, that says they will never be seen again. That one was a minister, he finished up at the end of a rope. This one is a dissident, he succumbed under torture. There were legions of them rotting in my dungeons, there for not having been worthy of my trust or my charity. They were my enemies. They only got what they deserved. But the people, my people, that mass I made with my own hands, that I gave birth to with forceps as I bit my lips, that I boosted in every one of my speeches and raised in the community of nations, what malignancy possessed it so that from one day to the next, without warning, it discarded what I had built for it and decided to crucify me on my own pedestal?

I have no regrets about clamping down.

It was legitimate and necessary.

A guide, though entrusted with a messianic mission, when he has official responsibility for a country, does not turn the other cheek. Quite the opposite: if he wants to fulfil his function properly, he must cut off the hand that was raised against him, even if the slap came from his father. From that perspective my conscience is clear, I am satisfied that I carried out my duty. I have killed, tortured, terrorised, hunted down, decimated families – because I had no alternative. But I did no wrong to the innocent. I only punished the guilty, the traitors and spies. I am ready to confront them on the day of reckoning and I shall make them bow their heads because they were at fault … Will the people have the audacity to look me in the face in God's house? What will they have to say when they are asked, 'What have you done with our elected one?' … Words will fail them, just as the courage to look me in the eyes will fail them. The Devil take repentance when it produces damnation. He who burns his bridges burns every chance of forgiveness. Libya will never see the day light its way again; nowhere will it bask in sunshine, because darkness is its destiny.

Suddenly, a cracking noise … some pebbles clatter into the ditch, then a shadow falls across the circle of light at the end of the tunnel. I make out a weapon first, then a head leaning in … He's here! I've found him! He's here, sir … Running steps return. Rebels spring into the ditch, their weapons aimed at me. They do not dare come any nearer and remain some distance away, startled and indecisive.

An individual in paramilitary uniform jumps down.

'Where is he?'

'In there, sir. He's crouched down at the end, on the left.'

The commander takes off his helmet and looks at me in silence.

'I can't believe my eyes,' he exclaims. 'Is it really you or is it your twin?'

He takes a step forward, then another, with all the caution of a mine clearance expert. He is afraid to come closer, and lowers his head as if he cannot believe his eyes. It takes him some time to be certain that he is not hallucinating.

'No, it's really him,' he shouts. 'It's really Muammar Gaddafi. Only he could end up like this: making like a rat … like a sewer rat at the bottom of a drain.'

Behind him men pass the word back: It's Gaddafi … it's Gaddafi …

The commander opens his arms.

'I wouldn't have missed this for the world. What a picture! What a moral! The man who thought he could ride the clouds is trapped in an old drainpipe … You've gone back to your roots, Brotherly Guide. You were born out of camel dung and you're going to die in your own shit … Amr,' he yells at one of his companions, 'get your mobile out and film this exceptional curtain call for me.'

Shadows start to mill around the mouth of the tunnel. Mobile phones are held up to immortalise the scene.

The commander allows several flashes to streak the tunnel before raising his hand to put an end to the ritual. He crooks his finger to order me to join him.

'Get your carcass over here, Brotherly Guide. I can't wait to squeeze you in my arms so tight I'll have you pissing out of your arse.'

His crudity shocks me, more than my capture.

'Come and get me,' I challenge him.

'Just watch me.'

'He might be armed,' a rebel warns, taking aim at me.

'The Brotherly Guide doesn't need to burden himself with weapons,' the commander says. 'The Force is with him.'

Sardonic laughter greets the leader's sarcasm, followed by a whole squad of men lunging at me. I feel as if I am coming apart.

They push and drag me out of the pipe. Armed men encircle me in a cosmic silence. They are stock-still, transfixed with incredulity. For a good many of them it must be the first time they have seen me so close to. They think they are seeing things. If I happened to clear my throat, I am almost convinced they would run away without a backward glance. The majority of my captors are boys not much taller than their guns; they look utterly ridiculous in their would-be fighters' uniforms. Some of them look away, unable to hold my gaze; others find it difficult to control their facial expressions.

Alerted to my capture, groups of rebels start running up and firing in the air to get the party started. Allāhu Akbar ... death to the *taghut* ... Oussoud Misrata, lions of Misrata ... Within minutes more than a hundred of them are crowding around me, elbowing each other hard to get closer to the strange creature in their midst.

They jostle me across the fields, they spit on me, they promise me the most violent treatment. I lose a shoe, stumble on stones, keep going under the battering of rifle butts ...

One hairy weirdo surges up in front of me, slapping my face as he does so.

I smile at him.

'I forgive you.'

'I don't, fucking madman. No one here forgives you.'

'What did he say?' someone asks behind me.

'He forgives us.'

'He's got a nerve. He still thinks he's The Exceedingly Merciful.'

Tongues loosen, jeering and gibes pour out of them, and like a bush fire the uproar spreads and multiplies into shouting, demands for my death, turning into bedlam and booming pandemonium. A thousand howler monkeys swarm at me in a spate of saliva. All I can see are foaming mouths bellowing at me, bloodshot eyes, hands trying to tear me limb from limb. The men escorting me are overwhelmed. They punch out with flailing fists at their comrades to keep them away from me, but to no avail. The commander vainly orders his troops to keep back; he has no control over them. In the general frenzy, woe to anyone who stumbles. I try to walk upright, with my head high, as my rank and quality demand, but the brambles have set my shoeless foot on fire, forcing me to hop. That's right, you son of a bitch, jump like you're playing hopscotch … What's the matter with him? Have his plush carpets made him forget the softness of our nourishing earth? … I want to tear his balls off and keep them in formalin ... Why don't we hang him? What are we waiting for? ... He deserves to have his throat cut in a drain ... We should douse him in petrol and set him on fire ... Dog ... fucker ... filthy bastard ... In the frenzy swarming around me, I see only hatred and curses. Faces blend into each other in a chaotic swell topped with the poisonous foam of the whites of their eyes. My turban is torn off and a thousand hands rain down on my skull; a leg of my trousers is torn off and a thousand hands pinch my backside and defile my private parts; my hair is torn out, I am bespattered with spit continuously, a thousand foul throats demand my death.

I refuse to acknowledge what is happening to me; it is a bad dream. Everything about it is absurd, exaggerated, incongruous; it seems the work of surrealists. Are these hideous faces yelling their filth at me really human? And how are these tentacle-like arms, which seem to be surging towards me out of the darkness, able to reach me in the tangled forest that binds me? ... Show yourself, van Gogh. For the love of your art, show yourself, so I can wake up with a start, and go back to the cosy splendour of my palaces, my obsequious servants and my enchanted harems ... Van Gogh is nowhere to be seen. I am not dreaming. My nightmare is as real as the blood on my forehead. I did not feel the rifle butt that split my skull. In fact I feel nothing any more. I have a confused sensation of what is taking place, a bizarre feeling of detaching myself from one reality and emerging into another where I have no point of reference. I feel as if the shot of heroin I was given last night is finally starting to have an effect. I am levitating, borne upwards by the savagery of a people I so cherished and who are getting ready to tear me apart with their bare hands.

The uproar of voices swirls around me. I feel woozy. A wreck tossed by angry waves. Let's tie him to the pickup and drag him behind it till his flesh and the road become one. Blows and insults beat down on me relentlessly. I do not defend myself. Muffled inside my stupor, I let myself drift towards my fate, my head crowned with thorns, my face covered in blood like Isa Ibn Maryam, bowed under his cross on the path to Golgotha.

I am not afraid.

My feelings are dulled.

I have a vague sensation that I am gravitating to the edge of things, that all my senses have deserted me.

They throw me in the back of a pickup, which has trouble forcing its way through the tumult. Its horn reverberates inside me like the trumpets of the Revelation. I am no longer of flesh and blood, I am tragedy, I am the putting to death itself. I do not even pity this people any longer, running to their doom while they imagine they are catching up with the pickup transporting me to further furies.

The vehicle halts. Wild hordes block its path, overwhelm it. I am grabbed, torn apart and then served up to dogs and villains. Talons tear off my clothes and the skin with it. Someone thrusts a bayonet into my anus. The lynching begins; this time it is the real thing. They strip me, they skin me alive, they eat me raw. I do not resist, I let myself be cut to pieces without a groan or entreaty to anyone, stoical and dignified, just as the old lion accepts his fate as the hyenas tear him apart. The stampede reaches its peak. Flocks of vultures fight over my body. Take it, I give it to you willingly; tear it to pieces, dissect it; you have a right to my limbs, to my organs, to my sinews, but my spirit will outlive you. Your howls glorify me; my torment is my salvation. Only exceptional beings finish this way, merging with the crowd. The intensity of the blows redoubles; now that I am completely naked, hands rummage in my genitals, tear out the hair in handfuls, fiddle with my penis, pluck at my testicles, claw at my back, penetrate my rectum; I feel nothing, I am beyond the reach of the lynch mob and their cannibalistic desires. Purged of all toxins, I no longer feel anger or hate. I belong to the Spirit that doubts not, that nothing can surprise and that cannot feel anger, for anger is an admission of weakness, and which is the god that would falter before human foolishness? I have passed beyond the state of humankind, of those perishable beings shaped by pride and error. I bequeath them my mortal remains to act as a reminder of their own woes and, purged of all fears and restraints, I prepare to fly to that eternal heaven, my sins washed away with my blood, expiated with my final breath, for I die as a martyr to be reborn in legend. I am no longer a rais, I am a prophet; my downfall is my fertiliser, for in the future to come I shall grow higher than the mountains.

Suddenly, in the midst of the storm, looking up, I see the sky above the repulsive masks salivating over me. For a fraction of a second it seems to me that the full moon has taken the place of the sun. In a final momentary revival, I offer a prayer at random: Lord, forgive them their sins as I forgive them, for they do not know what they do … A gunshot goes off. Point blank. It is for me. My *coup de grâce*. The Lord has decided to cut short my agony. I knew He would not abandon me. God does not desert His elected; He makes of their end the beginning of a new faith, of their suffering a proof of transcendence … I fall in slow motion to the ground, freed of my ties, relieved of my wrongdoings, delivered from my remorse; I am born again from my wounds, new like a soul who has just emerged from his mother's womb. Slowly the cries fade one after another, then the faces, then the daylight. I am dying, but my stamp will remain. For having left my imprint on their consciousness, my reward is to live on in the memory of peoples, to surf the ages that will race at top speed towards the infinite, to bombard them with remembrance of me until History becomes my pyramid. I shall be missed; I shall be sung in schools; my name shall be engraved on the marble of stelae and sanctified in the mosques; the epic of my life shall inspire poets and playwrights; painters shall devote frescoes to me wider than the horizon; I shall be venerated, wept over at the moment of repentance, and I shall have as many saints as accomplices, as is fitting for exceptional guides.

I make my bow; I am already on the other side of things and living beings, there where no sacrilege is to be found, where no mistake or misunderstanding can make me believe that the love of a people is an unfailing oath that cannot be broken …

My soul is leaving my body.

I float above the dust, see the ambulance forcing its way through the mob to take me to who knows what horror show, see the rebels revelling in their ignoble ritual, others brandishing pieces of my bloody clothing; I see tyre marks on the tarmac, the breeches of weapons glinting in the sun, the rebel banners flapping in the wind, but I do not hear the din of their jubilation or the noise of the volleys as they fire into the air in exultation.

I see everything: the sweat on faces as tense as if they have cramp, the eyes rolling upwards, the thick foam at the corners of their mouths, the crowd congratulating itself non-stop, the voyeurs immortalising with their mobiles the moment of their spiralling descent, but I cannot hear anything, not even the cosmic breath that is breathing me in.

It is now that my mother summons me, from across all these mirages. Her voice reaches me from the depths of a Fezzan eaten away by the desert. I see her again, her head in her hands, angry at my wild, boyish mischievousness: You only listen with one ear, the one you willingly lend to your devils, while the other is deaf to all reason … And it is at that precise moment, just before I dissolve among the swirls of nothingness, that I understand why that diabolical van Gogh, with his mutilated ear, broke in on my nights and on my madness.

But it is too late.